Horsefeathers

Horse Cents

Dandi Daley Mackall

DISCARD

Horsefeathers

Horsefeathers!
Horse Cents
Horse Whispers in the Air
A Horse of a Different Color

Interest level: ages 12–16

All Scripture quotations are taken from the HOLY BIBLE, NEW INTERNATIONAL VERSION®. NIV®. Copyright © 1973, 1978, 1984 by International Bible Society. Used by permission of Zondervan Publishing House. All rights reserved.

Text copyright © 2000 Dandi Daley Mackall
Published by Concordia Publishing House
3558 S. Jefferson Avenue, St. Louis, MO 63118-3968
Manufactured in the United States of America

1 2 3 4 5 6 7 8 9 10   09 08 07 06 05 04 03 02 01 00

*I dedicate this book to my parents, who
endured my extreme horse-craziness
and let Maureen and me ride our way
through childhood.*

Nothing smells better than fresh straw, barn air, and horse—my horse. Orphan nickered and nodded at me, tossing her wavy, black mane like a woman showing off her hair in a shampoo commercial.

"You know, Orphan," I said, heaving the last pitchfork of manure out of her stall, "if I could live anywhere in the whole world, I'd live right here in this very stall at Horsefeathers."

Morning sunlight filtered in through barn cracks, marking the stable from loft to floor with bright, dancing stripes. "Only I'd be a horse just like you," I added. I grabbed straw from the pile and sprinkled it over the cleaned stall. "Horse-feathers Stable has got to be the most peaceful spot on God's green—"

"Scoop! Help!" Maggie's cry pierced the calm barn like a sonic boom. "Scoop! Get out here! That crazy horse is going to hurt Moby!"

I dropped my armload of straw and ran outside. *Horsefeathers!* I should have known the peace

5

was too good to last. Straw stuck to my sweaty arms and neck as I raced to the paddock.

Maggie was waving her pink cowboy hat over the paddock fence at the two horses, who snorted and squealed at each other. Dust swirled around their stamping hooves. Ham, Carla Buckingham's beautiful bay gelding, bared his teeth at Maggie's old horse, Moby.

I sensed what was coming. But before I could holler, Ham tucked his head, swiveled around, and kicked. Moby grunted as the blow landed on her haunch.

I leaped the fence, catching my shirt and scraping my elbow on the way over. I heard something rip as I landed boots first on the hard, cracked paddock ground. The last thing I needed was to get myself in the middle of a horse fight. But the last thing Maggie's 23-year-old mare needed was to get another kick—especially in *my* stable.

"Come on, guys," I said, moving in on Ham. He flattened his ears back. "Did you forget our motto? This isn't what I had in mind by ... *where a horse can be a horse.*"

Horsefeathers Stable had been my dream come true. Actually, more like my prayer come true. I'd taken over what used to be Grandad's horse farm and turned it into a home for *backyard horses*. That's what Maggie and I have always called our horses. We grew up with them—in our backyards. Our horses aren't just animals to ride in horse shows or competitions. Moby and Orphan are our friends.

Only Carla Buckingham's horse, Ham, hadn't been very friendly lately. Even Orphan hadn't made friends with Ham. And my mare is everybody's friend.

"Easy, Ham," I said, stumbling over a crack in the gray earth. The bay jolted back a stride. The acrid smell of horse sweat and panic came at me in a wave through the dust of the paddock.

"Ham wasn't this bad when he moved in," I whispered to Maggie. "He's just turned spooky this past week or so. I think it's Carla's fault. She's been so nervous lately, Ham picks up on it. Move on down the fence, Maggie, and call Moby."

Glancing at Ham, I read quiet terror in the white around his tiny, dark pupils. "Don't be afraid, Ham," I murmured. "Moby won't hurt you."

"Scoop! Moby hurt *him*?" Maggie cried. Dressed in a pink, fringed Western shirt and matching skirt, Maggie Brown looked more like a cowgirl doll than a cowgirl. If Maggie were a horse, she'd be an Appaloosa, a one-of-a-kind. Appies come in all varieties of colors and markings—no two exactly alike, like snowflakes. Like Maggie Brown.

Maggie whistled, and her big white mare came instantly. "I won't let that high-class, stuck-up horse hurt *you*, Moby," she said dramatically.

Moby put her head over the fence and let

Maggie scratch her ears and finger-comb her long, full, white forelock.

Orphan trotted over to Moby and nuzzled her. As worried as I was about Ham, I couldn't help feeling a wave of gratitude and pride. Orphan and Moby were my black-and-white pasture partners. They spent hours every day grazing side by side or standing close, their necks entwined in a mutual back scratch. Their friendship was exactly what I'd pictured when I'd dreamed about running my own stable.

"Aren't you supposed to gentle horses here at Horsefeathers, Scoop?" Maggie asked, her big, brown eyes narrowed to slivers. She shot Ham a dirty look. "Better tell that horse he's going to ruin your reputation as a teenaged horse whisperer."

"Horsefeathers, Maggie," I said, taking a step toward Ham. "He'll come around." I hoped I sounded more confident than I felt. Ham is highstrung, but for the last week something had come over him that couldn't be explained by his American Saddle Horse temperament. He was skittish as a green colt.

Behind me I heard Maggie groan. "Give me a break," she said. "What are *you* doing here, Stephen? Go back to your own stables where you belong."

Not Stephen Dalton. And just when I thought things couldn't get much worse. Stephen and his dad own Dalton Stables, the ritziest stable in the county. They'd done everything they could to keep me from getting Grandad's barn and starting up Horsefeathers Stable. Usually I can tell right away what kind of horse a person would be if he were a horse. But not Stephen. No way he'd ever be a horse. Maybe a jackal or a hyena on a bad day.

I peeked over my shoulder and glimpsed his slicked-down red hair and permanent scowl. His pea-green eyes were slits as he looked down his nose at Horsefeathers. And he wasn't alone. I didn't recognize the tall, slim blond with him, but she looked about our age—14 or 15. Probably a boarder at Dalton Stables. She had that Dalton sneer down pat.

"Looks like you could use some help, Sarah Coop!" Stephen called.

That's my real name—Sarah Coop—S. Coop. But Stephen Dalton is just about the only person who uses it. And he uses it to make me mad. I think Grandad started calling me Scoop when I was 3 and my folks adopted me. I didn't talk. Dotty, the aunt I live with now, claims the first word I said was "Orphan," and the second was "Scoop!"—meaning, "Scoop me up and put me on that horse."

Stephen's mom and my adopted dad were brother and sister, so we have the same grandad in common—but nothing else. I ignored Stephen and focused on Ham.

Turning sideways to the bay, I murmured

sweet nothings to him until he gave in and shuffled over to me. When he did, I scratched his neck and felt his muscles relax. "You're just a loner, aren't you, Fella," I said, understanding probably a lot better than Maggie and Stephen about being alone. I led Ham to the side pasture and closed the gate so he could stay by himself for a night.

People say I've got horse sense. All I know is that to me, horses make a lot more sense than people.

"Is Moby okay?" I asked, jogging over to Maggie to check out her mare's injury.

"Okay?" Maggie repeated. "How would you feel if that beast kicked you?" Maggie plans to be an actress, so it's hard to get a straight answer out of her.

I ran my fingers down Moby's haunch. She didn't flinch or quiver, even when I picked up her back hoof. The nick from Ham's unshod hoof was the size of a fingernail.

"She's fine, Maggie," I said. I let go of Moby's back leg, but didn't move fast enough to get clear of her hoof. She stomped me good, catching three of my toes.

"Ouch!" I cried, pushing Moby off my boot. Moby backed into Orphan, who bumped Maggie off the fence. She twirled like a ballerina.

Stephen and his girlfriend stared at us like we were part of the circus. The girl looked even taller up close, next to my 5'4" height. If she'd been a horse, she'd have been a Hackney, long, lean, and high-stepping. Her blond hair was perfectly straight, parted on the side so it dangled over one eye. I could only see one eyebrow, and it had been plucked to look like a tiny comma.

Her perfume smelled so expensive that all of a sudden I realized what I must smell like and look like to her. Dust and manure covered my jeans. I'd ripped my sleeveless, plaid shirt halfway up one side. My dust-colored hair was only half in the braid it started in this morning.

"Ursula," Stephen said between snickering noises, "isn't Horsefeathers everything I promised you?"

Ursula burst into laughter and gave Stephen's shoulder a feminine push. "Stephen, stop! You are *so* funny!" Maggie would have called Ursula's voice sexy, but I thought she sounded hoarse. She craned her long neck in all directions, lightly touching the collar on her high-necked, white silk shirt that might have cost a month's boarding fees at Horsefeathers. "Where are the rest of the horses?"

"You're looking at them," Stephen said. "No kidding. This is it. All of it."

Maggie wheedled her way between them. "Obviously, you've been misinformed. So far—and we are *just* beginning—Horsefeathers Stable is home to these three horses *and* Cheyenne, that gorgeous Paint out there." Maggie pointed to the back pasture, where Cheyenne was drinking at the pond. "We wanted to form a secure base—four girls, four horses. Then we'll have to start accepting some of the people who've been begging to board their horses here. Scoop is the only horse whisperer in this part of the country. She *gentles* horses ..." Maggie turned to Steven. "... unlike other stables we could mention, where horses are *broken*."

Maggie flashed her famous Maggie smile at the girl. "So if you're here about renting a stall for your horse, I'm sorry to disappoint you ... Ursula, is it?"

Maggie is like a verbal tornado. I'm always grateful when she's around to talk for me. We could have used several new boarders, but we both knew this Ursula wasn't looking to be one of them.

The girl gave Maggie a noncommittal nod and a two-second fake smile involving nothing but her lips, which, by the way, were four times as thick as Stephen's pencil-line mouth. I tried not to imagine them kissing, her pouty lips trying to find his.

"Ursula," Stephen said, his reddish hair suddenly making me think of rotten apples. "This one is Maggie Brown, the owner of the old white nag that—"

"Get it right, Stephen," Maggie said, taking Ursula's hand and giving it one firm shake. "Maggie 37 Rose is the name. My mother's lucky number is 37, and I was born in the third month, on the seventh day, and that explains my middle name, more or less."

Maggie didn't bother explaining that although her middle name really is 37, she changes her last name as easily as she changes her clothes—and usually to the same color. She's always looking for the perfect stage name. When I'd seen her in her pink cowboy hat, I'd thought she might be trying out Maggie *Pink*, but Maggie *Rose* had a nicer ring to it.

Stephen put his arm around Ursula's shoulder, which made me cringe. He leaned into her and checked his watch. "Let's get back to Dalton Stables, shall we?" he said. "We can watch them work our horses on the lunge line about now." They turned their backs on Maggie and me.

"I do see what you mean about Horsefeathers Stable, Stephen," Ursula said, her voice deep and gravely. "I couldn't imagine leaving *my* show horse here."

"I'm glad we got to see Mrs. Buckingham's horse, though," Stephen said, louder than he had to. "Now we'll have something to tell her when she stops by Dalton Stables again."

Mrs. Buckingham? At Dalton Stables? When Carla Buckingham first moved to West Salem, her mother booked Buckingham's British Pride (Ham's official name) into Dalton Stables. But Carla had eventually convinced her mom to let Ham move to Horsefeathers.

Maggie and I exchanged looks. I knew Maggie personally would love to see Ham banished from Horsefeathers and kicked back to Dalton Stables. But even Maggie had to know we couldn't afford to lose a single boarding fee—not to mention what losing Buckingham's business might do to Horsefeathers' reputation ... and to mine.

Maggie was after them in a flash. "Wait up!" she called, her pink boots crunching the dirt as she stormed up to them. "What was Carla's mother doing at Dalton Stables?"

"Excuse me?" Ursula asked, looking down at Maggie in a way that made me wonder if she might be prejudiced against African Americans. "Are *you* speaking to *me*?"

I braced myself. Nobody gets the best of Maggie 37 Brown.

"Listen to me, you cross between Alice in Wonderland and Darth Vader," Maggie said. "It so happens I *am* speaking to—"

Stephen stepped between Ursula and Maggie. "Let me handle this, Ursula," he said. "Maggie, Mrs. Buckingham did come by Dalton Stables this morning, if you must know. She asked when we thought we'd have an opening. From what I understand, she's not sure *Horsemeat*—I mean, *Horsefeathers*—is right for a show horse like hers."

Ursula stuck her head over Stephen's shoulder. In the lowest voice yet she said, "I imagine that if Mrs. Buckingham wasn't sure before, she will be now."

Horsefeathers, Maggie!" I kicked up puffs of
dirt as I watched Ursula and Stephen prance
off arm in arm. "Now Mrs. Buckingham will
want to move Ham to Dalton Stables for sure!"

Staring back at Ham, I sent up a silent prayer
that we could keep him at Horsefeathers. I glanced
at Orphan and asked God why He put two-legged
creatures in charge of four-legged ones.

Maggie sighed and tucked in her pink, silky
shirt. "If it weren't for your reputation as a horse
gentler, I'd say good riddance to bad horses who
kick Moby." She lifted her pink cowboy hat and
skillfully removed two hairpins that freed her
beautiful, wavy brown hair. With one shake, her
hair bounced to her shoulders.

"Maggie, I don't even have a reputation to
ruin yet. In case you haven't noticed, people
aren't exactly pounding down the barn door to
get into Horsefeathers. We may need to scrounge
for another boarder just to meet this month's
bills. We sure can't afford to lose a boarder we
already have."

"Then you better figure out what's wrong with that horse," Maggie said.

"I know what's wrong with Ham, Maggie," I said. "I told you. It's Carla. She's edgy and worried about something. Her horse picks up on it even before she does."

"Then you better figure out what's wrong with Carla." Maggie glanced at her watch. "I've got to run to acting class. See ya, Scoop."

I watched Maggie as she biked down the lane, waving a hand in the air without turning around. Maggie 37 Brown is probably my best friend in the whole world, but she has zero horse sense.

Orphan bumped me from behind, nudging me with her nose.

I turned and lightly stroked her velvety muzzle. "Now *you've* got horse sense," I said. I hoisted myself up to sit on the top rail so Orphan could rest her head across my lap and get her ears scratched. "Orphan, we may be in big trouble. We've got to get Ham settled in, or we may lose him." I leaned my head against Orphan's and could have stayed like that all day.

After another minute, I kissed Orphan on her white blaze and hopped down. "Sorry, Girl. I've got to get to work. You know there's nothing I'd rather do than jump on you and take off to our secret spot. But duty calls."

I'd been giving Cheyenne two workouts a day to get her calmed for the Zucker family. Cheyenne belongs to Jen Zucker, who'd been great helping at Horsefeathers whenever she wasn't baby-sitting one of her eight siblings. Besides boarding their Paint at Horsefeathers, the Zuckers were paying me extra to "gentle" her. Cheyenne was 5 years old and had never been more than green broke.

For the next hour I ran Cheyenne through her paces and rode her into the pond to splash out some of her energy. At least something at Horsefeathers was going according to schedule. In her two weeks at my home for backyard horses, Cheyenne had learned to come when I called her, stand in cross-ties for grooming, take the bit without a fight, and only shy at things bigger than a breadbox.

On the other hand, Cheyenne couldn't stand to be in the same pasture as Ham. I had to keep them separated or we'd really have had a fight on our hands.

By the time I finished cooling down Cheyenne, it was almost 1:00. I was due at Carla's in 10 minutes. I'd promised to bring Ham with me so we could go riding in the woods behind Carla's house.

I threw a hackamore on Orphan, a kind of bitless bridle, and told her to wait while I tacked up Ham. Then I swung myself up on Orphan and set off bareback to Carla's, her horse in tow.

"Come on, Ham," I begged from the back of Orphan. Orphan tensed and kept looking back to see where Ham was. Ham stayed as far from us as the lead rope allowed. "Can't you two be friends?" I coaxed.

Carla had just moved to West Salem as school was ending our eighth-grade year. She and I had started off as enemies, but now I considered us good friends. Maybe there was still hope for Ham and Orphan.

Buckingham Palace, my nickname for Carla Buckingham's mansion, appeared over the treetops. It was the biggest house in the county, and already they were building an addition that looked bigger than my house.

The sun wove in and out of the clouds, giving me brief reprieves from the summer heat. Orphan snorted and arched her neck. Riding her bareback let me feel when her muscles tensed. "What's up, Orphan?" I murmured.

Orphan can pick up the scent of a deer or the sight of a chipmunk long before I can. I urged her closer to the house. Then I heard what had Orphan's ears twitching. Shouting. I pulled up a few feet from the house, but loud voices shot across the lawn in spurts, as if angry people were hurling them at a target—us.

"It's your fault we're in this dinky, lifeless town!" I'd only met Carla's mother twice. But she'd been shouting both times, and I didn't have any trouble recognizing her voice now. "There's not a theater or an orchestra within an hour of here! And the only operas any of these people can talk about are soap operas!"

"Sylvia! We agreed on this move. A 'fresh start' I believe you called it." It was a man's voice, probably Carla's dad.

I didn't want to eavesdrop, but I couldn't leave. Carla was expecting me.

"Oh yes, go ahead and blame me!" Mrs. Buckingham was screaming now. "That's all anyone around here does anymore. Well, I am sick and tired of it!"

I pictured Carla hiding under the bed. I hoped she didn't have her hearing aids in.

"Then you can fly off to Switzerland and leave me here to rot!" Mrs. Buckingham's voice was so loud that if I'd never seen her I might have pegged her for a Percheron mare. But in person, she's refined, as stylish as an Arabian.

"I was doing just fine in Kentucky. You're the one who wanted to go into private practice!" I'd never met Carla's dad, but yelling, he sounded kind of like a Brumby, the wild bush horse of Australia. "Just don't forget whose idea it was to buy this house!"

"My fault again, right? Of course! And who promised me the builder would have my office finished by now? All I do in this dump is stare at the walls all day and listen to the pounding and banging. And I baby-sit our daughter, who can't even hear what I'm saying half the time!"

Ever since Carla had moved to West Salem, I'd thought she had it made. I would have traded places with Carla Buckingham in a galloping second. Two parents to my none. And both of them lawyers who made more money in a year than Dotty could make in a lifetime at the grocery store.

Now I wasn't so sure I wanted to be in Carla's shoes. I don't remember my parents arguing like that. I hope they never did.

"Sylvia!" Carla's dad shouted. "Do you want Carla to hear you?"

"Frankly," her mother shouted back, "I don't know what I want! But I don't want this!" She stormed out onto the porch, slamming the door and barreling head down, off the porch, down the steps—

And right smack dab into Orphan.

"Horsefeathers!" I whispered.

3

Mrs. Buckingham glared up at me like an outraged Mustang mare ready to bite. "How long have you been standing there?" She sounded like a lawyer accusing me of a huge crime against the state.

"I ... uh ..." Maggie would have known what to say. "Carla told me ... told me to meet her ..." I couldn't get the words out.

Mrs. Buckingham frowned at Ham, who was pulling backwards on the lead like a balking donkey. It was all I could do to hang onto the lead rope and not be pulled off Orphan's rump.

"Why is he so nervous?" she asked. But she was asking the wrong person, and the question still sounded like a cross examination. "I don't like the way that horse has been behaving. Ever since he left Dalton Stables, he's turned jumpy. You know I was against moving him to Horsefeathers. I do not approve of a stable run by teenaged girls. And I haven't made any secret about how I feel."

She was right about that. Maybe my reputation as a horse *gentler* was in worse trouble than I thought. A giant shiver started at the base of my neck and traveled down my spine and out my toes. You'd have thought it was nine degrees out instead of 90.

Mrs. Buckingham walked back and stared at her champion bay. "I'll give your Horsefeathers Stable until the end of the month to get this horse settled. Do you understand? I'll not have that horse ruined. Do you have any idea how much Buckingham's British Pride is worth?"

I didn't, but I wasn't sure she wanted an answer. Some grown-ups ask a lot of questions they don't really want answered. Mrs. Buckingham probably thought Orphan wasn't worth much because I don't have papers on her. But to me, all horses are worth a whole lot more than papers or money. I knew for sure that wasn't the answer she was looking for either. I shrugged.

Sylvia Buckingham shook her head, then got in her black convertible and drove off, gravel crunching and spitting out from her back tires.

I let myself sink forward and wrap my arms around Orphan's neck. I needed to smell her, as much as people need smelling salts after they faint.

"Scoop!" Carla appeared on the porch, tugging her dad by his sleeve. I could tell by her smile she hadn't heard much of the argument. Not even Maggie could have acted normal after that scene.

I sent up a quick prayer of thanks that at least

Carla hadn't overheard what her mom said about her.

"You have to meet my father," Carla said, dragging him to the front of the porch. "This is Scoop, Father," Carla said. "Sarah Coop—the horse gentler I told you about? Wait till you see how she operates at Horsefeathers!"

It sounded more like, "*Way dill you see how she prates ah Horfedder.*" But I hardly noticed Carla's speech problems anymore. She'd explained to me that since she's never heard speech clearly, she doesn't speak clearly. Usually she just drops word endings, but when she gets emotional, she cuts out whole syllables. My mind learned pretty fast how to fill in the spaces between Carla's words.

Carla jumped from the porch and took Ham's lead rope. My fingers felt stiff from gripping the rope so tight. I opened and closed my fist, shaking out the tingles.

"Scoop, I'd like to present Edward Buckingham, III." Carla reached into her pocket and pulled out two things that looked like large, plastic beans—her hearing aids. She stuck one in each ear. So that explained how she'd missed the fight. She didn't have her hearing aids in. "Better meet my father while you can. He's not around much."

"Carla!" her dad scolded.

I nodded without looking him in the eyes. But a glance was enough to tell me he was no

23

wild Brumby horse. He had wavy brown hair and what Maggie might call a British flair—tall, stately, aristocratic. I was pretty sure nobody had ever called him Eddie or Ed. He'd have made a good Five-Gaited American Saddle Horse.

"I'm glad to meet you, Sarah," he said.

"*Scoop*, Father," Carla corrected. "Call her Scoop."

"Well, Scoop," he said, "your backyard horse stables must be agreeing with Buckingham's British Pride." He eyed the gelding from the porch. "I don't believe I've ever seen his coat so sleek."

I did a double-take to see if he was being sarcastic.

"*Ham*, Father," Carla corrected. "We're calling him Ham now." She stroked her gelding's perfectly muscled neck. "His coat *is* shiny, isn't it? It's the feed we use at Horsefeathers. And Scoop says Ham has been rolling in the dirt, so the loose hairs come off. Then he shines up great when we brush him."

"That's nice," said Edward Buckingham, III. He extended his arm and jerked up the sleeve of his dark, gray suit so he could see his Rolex. "You'll have to excuse me, Honey. I need to run to the bank. Very nice to meet you—"

"Scoop," I said, before he could call me Sarah again.

He drove off in a white, foreign-looking car that sounded like a motorcycle.

Carla stared after her dad just a minute too long. It made me think she might not be as cheery as she pretended to be. Then she wheeled around, grabbed the bridle I'd tied to Ham's saddle, and slipped it on her horse. In one smooth motion, she mounted her English saddle and found her right stirrup.

Carla looked calm enough to me, but Ham must have sensed something beneath her surface calm. Immediately the horse sidestepped, then pranced in place. Carla frowned and choked up on the reins, making Ham worse.

"Let's get out to the woods where we can all relax," I suggested, letting Orphan lead off.

Carla and Ham struggled with each other a couple of times, but in minutes we were deep into pine trees that shut us off from civilization. We might have been in a foreign country, miles from the nearest house. The firs grew skinny and straight. But when I squinted up at the sun, their straight, black trunks seemed to lean in together. Like teepee posts, the pines slanted to the sky, where they formed a small circle catching white flames of sunlight.

I was jerked back to the real world by Ham's grunt and the sliding thud of his hooves. "What's the matter?" I called back. I caught sight of Ham shying at something in the underbrush. His white-eyed fear was back.

"I think it was a rabbit," Carla said. "I wish he'd quit shying at every little thing."

"You know," I said, reaching up for a pine needle and smelling the minty resin, "horses won't relax if their riders don't."

"What are you saying, Scoop?" Carla snapped in a voice too much like her mother's.

"Nothing," I said. "Only horses have a sixth sense—horse sense, I guess. They feel what we're feeling—sometimes before we do. Did you know that touch is their sharpest sense? So when a rider's uptight, her horse—"

"Nobody's uptight," Carla said, cutting me off. "I'm just not used to riding for fun. And neither is Ham. We're usually too intent on practicing for the next horse show."

"You have to admit this beats riding in circles," I said, trying to lighten the tension that was closing in on us like a net. I liked working Cheyenne in the arena, and riding Ham there sometimes, and even Moby when Maggie had ballet or music classes. But this kind of free riding was what God had in mind when He made horses.

Carla took the lead down a side trail. Orphan's hooves were muffled in soft, brown pine needles. We followed the path east toward the pastures that connect the Buckingham fields with Grandad's back 40 and Horsefeathers. In a few minutes we'd left the trails for parched pasture ground. And the whole time, we'd never been farther than a few hundred yards away.

I ducked under a dead branch and came to a clearing filled with bright purple wildflowers. Somehow, even here where the grass ached for rain, the tiny balls of lavender held on.

Orphan sensed what I wanted and broke into a gentle canter. She made a breeze for both of us that wiped the sweat from my forehead.

Ham cantered too, a tight, neck-arched gait. He snorted at every stride as the wind blew the bay's thick, black tail straight out behind him. We reached the creek, dried to a skinny snake of brown water that Orphan sailed over without breaking stride. We slowed to a trot as Horse-feathers Stable came into view.

We were a pasture away when Orphan stopped and pricked up her ears. Ham did the same thing.

"What *is* that?" I asked, hearing, feeling, a thump-thumping. Some of the freedom I'd felt as Orphan sailed through the pasture and over the creek began to melt like an icicle struck by sunlight.

"You're asking me?" Carla cocked her head and tapped her hearing aid. "I *feel* music though."

We rode closer. The pounding beat grew louder and mixed with sounds I wouldn't call music. And it was definitely coming from Horse-feathers.

Orphan grew tense the closer we got, and Carla had her hands full with Ham. He got so wild she dismounted and led him in while Orphan and I rode ahead to the barn. Hard rock music blared so loud the barn floor vibrated. But I couldn't find where it was coming from.

Orphan followed me to the back of the barn. Moby was galloping to the far end of the pasture, and Cheyenne raced the back fence as if she planned on jumping it.

Carla and Ham walked up, both of them skittish. "It's even loud for me!" she shouted. I helped her tie Ham in the cross-ties and unbuckle his saddle. "It's coming from the roof, Scoop!" she shouted, pointing up.

The noise was so loud it might have been one long explosion. I ran back outside and looked up at the barn roof just in time to see a small figure creep behind the eaves.

"B.C.!" I screamed, knowing instantly my little brother had to be behind this. He was hiding behind the barn peak, but his tennis shoes stuck out and gave him away. "Bottle Cap Coop! I'm going to get you for this!"

I raced to the side of the barn, where a willow hung over the roof. In two seconds I shimmied up and made it to the rooftop. I spotted B.C.'s boom box and headed for it.

B.C. was only going into fourth grade, and already we'd gone through two psychiatrists to help him with manic depression, a disease that makes him almost like two different kids sometimes. He can be the sweetest, saddest, quietest kid—or an obnoxious monster. The doctors claim that B.C.'s depression isn't catching, but he depresses me sometimes.

I charged through invisible waves of rock noise until I reached the boom box and hit the off button.

The silence was wonderful, like a toothache that quit hurting.

"Hey! Turn it back on!" B.C. appeared in blue jean shorts and a ratty T-shirt. He's small for his age, but with his teeth bared, he looked like an angry old man, a miniature version of my grandfather.

"You little brat!" I screamed, my voice louder in the empty air. "Your horrible music scared the horses so much I probably won't be able to work them the rest of the day!"

B.C. reached into his pocket, pulled out a bottle cap and zinged it at me. I ducked and felt it whiz over my head. I wheeled around in time to see the metal cap land at Cheyenne's hooves. She jumped out of the way.

"Now look what you did!" I scolded. "What's the matter with you?" I was shaking from rage. "You shouldn't even be here. Dotty told you to stay with Grandad. Go home, B.C.!"

"You're not the boss of me!" screamed B.C., his brown eyes almost as wide as Ham's.

Before I could stop him, he grabbed his boom box and slid down the tree. By the time I climbed down after him, he'd disappeared. "B.C.!" I yelled into the pasture.

Orphan came up to console me.

"Scoop! Come here! Quick!" Carla's yell came from the other side of the barn.

What now? I tore through the barn toward the paddock, expecting to see—I'm not sure what I expected. A major horse fight? B.C. setting the barn on fire? Flaming horsefeathers!

4

Carla yelled something else I couldn't make out. I dashed straight through Orphan's stall to the paddock. "What's going—"

Suddenly my feet slid out from under me. I landed splat in mud! *Mud?* It hadn't rained in two weeks. So why was I skidding on my side through a muddy paddock?

Carla screamed at me from the paddock fence. "B.C. ... water ... where?"

B.C.! I should have known he was behind this mess.

I tried to get up, but my boots slipped. I flipped myself over onto my stomach and managed to pull myself up to my hands and knees. A picture flashed through my mind of when B.C. was a little kid and I gave him horsey rides—me on my hands and knees just like this. I should have thrown him when I had the chance. Steadying myself, still in horsey position, I looked around me. Half of the paddock had turned into pure, black mud, spotted with puddles.

Whoosh. The swishing noise came from behind me. I glanced over my left shoulder to see what it was. A cold, hard flush of water hit me in the face. Water gushed up my nose, and stung my eyes.

Just as suddenly, the water stopped hitting me. I swiped at my eyes with the back of my muddy arm. I'd scrambled halfway to my feet when the water slashed across me again and knocked me back down.

That time I saw where it came from. A green snake of a hose danced wildly with a life of its own. It was Grandad's high-pressure fire hose.

Dodging the spray, I sloshed toward the hose and made a grab for it. The monster dived out of reach.

"I got it!" Carla yelled from somewhere near the barn.

The water cut off, and the snake died, plopping to the ground and burying itself in the mud it had created.

As soon as I caught my breath, I let out a wail: *"Beeeeeee Ceeeeee!"*

The only answer was the faint pounding of his music fading into the woods across the far pasture.

"He must have turned that hose on an hour ago!" I cried. "What does *he* care that I have to pay for that water? I'll make him pay for it out of his allowance. Out of his hide!" I tried to dry my face with a Kleenex, but it shredded all over my forehead.

Carla looked like she was trying not to laugh. "I ... I'll go find some rags to help you clean up," she said. My muddy shirt stuck to me, and my hair felt as if it had gained five pounds of mud.

Carla came back with a pan of water and clean rags. Then she did the best she could on my face and arms while I railed against B.C. "Brothers! Why me? Why didn't my folks leave well enough alone after they adopted me? First he scares the horses with his horrible so-called music. Then he ruins the paddock and runs up the water bill."

Orphan whinnied from her stall. I'd forgotten all about her. She'd been waiting patiently for me through the whole mess.

"Sorry, Orphan," I said, going to her and scratching her withers. "It's all B.C.'s fault."

The least I could do was give Orphan a good brushing. I grabbed the soft brush and started high on her neck under her mane. As I stroked her, some of my anger began to seep out.

Carla picked up another brush and worked on the opposite side.

"You know," I said, smoothing the soft hairs under Orphan's mane, "B.C. is a bratty Shetland Pony. I never know what he'll do next. I have no privacy. The other day, I found bottle caps in my pajama drawer!"

Carla laughed so hard Orphan craned her neck around to see. I hadn't seen Carla laugh for days.

"Go ahead and laugh," I said, brushing harder, making Orphan's sunburned coat shine reddish black. "You have no idea how lucky you are to be an only child, Carla."

Carla changed moods like a stoplight. Her laughter died. I couldn't even hear her breathing. Then she said softly, "I don't feel lucky." She groomed Orphan's long, black tail, the brush swishing a steady rhythm. "I like your brother, Scoop." She said it so low I almost didn't hear her.

"Excuse me?" I said, standing on tiptoes so I could see her over Orphan's back. "May I please borrow your hearing aids? I thought you said you like B.C." I cocked my head and tapped at my ear the way Carla does sometimes.

Carla laughed. We brushed quietly for a while, then she asked, "Why do you call him B.C.? I figured the *C* was for Coop."

"You figured wrong." Orphan stamped her hind hoof. "I'm getting there," I told her. "B.C. stands for Bottle Cap. We've called him B.C. since he was 2."

"Go on, Scoop," Carla urged when I fell silent. "What's the deal with the bottle caps? Where did he get them? Why does he carry them around?"

I couldn't believe she wanted to know this stuff. It was about the last thing I wanted to talk about. I didn't even know where to start. "Okay. You know I was adopted, right?"

Carla stopped brushing and nodded.

"Then my folks had B.C. the regular way— which I'm sure they never would have done if they'd known how rotten he was going to turn out."

"Scoop! Go on—"

I sighed almost the same minute Orphan did. "See, our folks worked in the bottle plant on different shifts. Every night my dad used to come home after dark and dump a pocketful of bottle caps at B.C.'s bare feet. B.C. would hear the groan of the front porch step, the one Dad never got around to fixing. And the kid would act like Santa Claus was out there."

Orphan sneezed, spraying my arm. "Thanks, Orphan," I said, wiping it on my muddy jeans.

"Go on," Carla said, still not brushing.

"My brother had a whole corner of his room piled to the ceiling with bottle caps. He'd plow the bottle cap mountain with toy trucks. Later, he used bottle caps as army men. It's still about all he plays with. Only now, he builds things with bottle caps."

I didn't feel like talking about it any more. "So there you have it—the mystery of B.C. On the other hand, maybe *B.C.* stands for *Big Creep*."

Carla didn't laugh. She must have figured she was done with her half of the brushing. The only sound came from my brush as I finished Orphan's back leg.

Carla asked, "Scoop, how did they die ... your parents?"

Orphan looked back at me with her big, brown eyes, as if she could read how hard this was for me. I never talk about my parents. Even though they've been dead for seven years, it still hurts to talk about them. So I don't. Not unless I'm cornered.

"Please, Scoop?" Carla asked.

"The bottle plant blew up and killed both of them," I said, giving her the end of the story so I wouldn't have to drag it out. It had been a freak accident—the explosion, and the fact that both of my parents had been in it even though they worked different shifts. Mom had gone in early so she wouldn't miss Dad.

I could still remember waking up in the dark—maybe by the sound of the explosion. Murmurs and whispers drifted up from the kitchen through the radiator grill. But I couldn't understand what they were saying.

I remember thinking B.C.'s bottle caps had come to life and were talking in a bottle-cap language only he could understand. I wanted to get out of bed and wake up B.C. so he could tell me what the voices were saying. But I couldn't keep my eyes open. So I just went back to sleep. I wish I could have stayed awake. I should have gotten up right then. I shouldn't have just gone back to sleep.

When I woke up, Dotty was there with breakfast. And I was an orphan again.

"Did they ... " Carla looked down at her boots. "Did they love each other a lot?"

I shrugged. "I guess." It wasn't something I'd ever thought about. Not like that. They were married. They took care of me and B.C. They must have been in love.

"I'm sorry, Scoop," Carla said. "I probably shouldn't have asked so many questions."

"It hasn't been so bad living with Dotty," I said. "She's okay." I'd only seen my aunt twice before she showed up that morning in the kitchen. At first I didn't even know who she was. She was just there taking care of things, and there she stayed.

"I'll bet it's really helped that you have a brother," Carla said.

I snorted. "Yeah, right," I said sarcastically, slipping a halter on Orphan. "B.C.'s been a real help all right."

Orphan followed me out of the barn. I opened the paddock gate and turned her out to pasture. Moby ran up to greet her. They blew gentle greetings at each other. Then they trotted to a bare spot, where Orphan kneeled, then dropped to the dirt for a good, hard roll. Moby followed suit, and the two of them rolled over and over until they were good and dirty.

Carla joined me. "Moby and Orphan are like

sisters, aren't they? I wish Ham didn't act like an only child."

Something about the way she said it seemed so sad. "Carla, are you okay? I mean, you're tense and—"

She cut me off. "Shouldn't you get home to your grandfather? You don't know if B.C. went back home or not."

"Horsefeathers," I muttered. "You're right. Who knows what Grandad might get into home alone all day. Yesterday he flushed his hairbrush, comb, toothpaste, and toothbrush down the toilet so nobody else would use them. Dotty thought she'd never get the toilet unclogged. I don't know who's worse—B.C. or Grandad."

"Go!" Carla commanded. "I'll finish up here. Are we still on for tonight? The Horsefeathers meeting?"

I'd almost forgotten. Jen had called the meeting to talk about our Horsefeathers' budget. I didn't think it would be good news. "I'll be here. Call Maggie and remind her, will you? Seven o'clock!" I took off down the lane. "Thanks!" I called over my shoulder.

Carla waved at me. When I got to the end of the lane, I looked back. She was standing in exactly the same spot, her arms wrapped around her.

The closer I got to home, the more worried I got about Grandad. B.C.'s fault again. He should have had enough sense to stay home instead of causing trouble at Horsefeathers. Too bad my dad hadn't given his son pocketfuls of horse sense instead of bottle caps.

By the time I reached our driveway, my jogging had turned to a dead heat run. I had a strong feeling I wasn't going to like what I was coming home to. Without stopping, I crossed the lawn to the side of the house. I stood still for a minute, catching my breath at the kitchen door. I put my hand on the doorknob and started to kick off my boots.

That's when I noticed water trickling over my toe. It was coming from under the door.

I flung open the door. A three-inch tidal wave flooded out. Our kitchen floor had been turned into a linoleum lake. Plastic cereal bowls floated upside down. A box of Hy-Klas cereal drifted by me, trailing soggy bran flakes in its wake. Rushing water poured from the faucet into the full sink and over the chipped, white enamel, where it formed a kitchen waterfall.

I sloshed to the sink and shut off the water. "B.C.!" I screamed. "Grandad! Anybody?"

Leaning against the wet counter, I pulled off my socks and splashed to the living room.

The gold-and-brown speckled shag carpet felt soggy. Luckily, our broken-down house slopes toward the back door instead of the front, so most of the water had stayed in the kitchen.

Grandad sat rocking in his wooden rocker. The chair's usual *squeak-squeak* had added a sloshy sound to the beat: *squeak-squish, squeak-squish.* My grandfather stared wide-eyed at the blank TV screen, as if he were watching a high-speed car chase.

I glanced from Grandad to the TV and back to Grandad. His red flannel shirt looked soaked clear through.

I thought about telling him to get in the kitchen and clean up his mess. I thought about reminding him that this wasn't *his* house and that we were the only thing standing between him and the funny farm. I thought about picking up the phone and calling Ralph Dalton to come get his father-in-law and drive directly to the nursing home—do not pass go—do not collect $200.

"You left the water on," I said. "You better change your shirt."

Grandad got up. His back stayed in the curved form of the rocker as he shuffled over to me. When I used to stare up at him, he'd seemed so tall. I'd felt that same awe I feel when I ride Orphan through the woods and stare up through the lean, tall trees at the sun. Now Grandad and I were barely eye to eye when he unbent his back.

Eyes as blank as the TV screen frowned at me. Suddenly he turned and shuffled away. He slipped into B.C.'s room, which he'd taken over when he moved in.

"Horsefeathers," I mumbled to the empty, waterlogged house. I headed for the kitchen and the mess I didn't make.

Most of the water had gone down, like low tide, seeped under the screen door. Bits of paper floated to the back door and stuck there. Other wads or strips clung to the kitchen's gray linoleum squares, as if they were waiting for lifeboats.

I picked up the paper wad closest to me. The soaked, wrinkled strip had been torn roughly on all sides. I could make out faint pencil marks and some of the letters written on it:

—*rovber*—then some numbers.

A sentence had been scrawled after that. It looked like Dotty's handwriting, but I couldn't make it out. I stepped toward the door to retrieve another piece of paper. My foot slipped, but I caught myself on the kitchen table. This note wasn't too wet to read, but it looked like part of it was missing. It said: *no one who understands, no one—*

"No kidding," I said out loud. But why would my aunt write it? It sure didn't sound like Dotty.

I collected all the strips of paper I could and set them out on a towel over the kitchen table. Then I went to work.

I wiped up water, muttering to myself the whole time as I tried to soak up the Pacific Ocean with a dishrag. Then I gave up and switched to the broom, sweeping water out the door. By 6:00, the floor seemed pretty dry. But my anger was still bursting at the floodgates.

The screen door slapped open and Dotty, her arms full of Hy-Klas plastic bags, shouldered her way in. She wore black pants and the orange apron everybody who worked at Hy-Klas had to wear. The people who invented the one-size-fits-all top never met my stocky aunt.

"Lookie here who I done found on the roof!" Dotty said. Her short leg stretched behind her to keep the door open. The fake crease down the front of her pantleg twisted and bunched. Brown glasses sat crooked on her broad nose, and her short, thin brown hair looked as if it must have been a hot day at the grocery store.

Still, all Dotty had to do was step into the kitchen and some of my anger fizzled out. Without even opening her mouth, Dotty reminds you of God.

I grabbed a couple of bags out of her arms.

B.C. darted in behind her.

My anger came galloping back. "You little—" I glanced at Dotty and changed words. "—brat!" I cut off B.C.'s escape route to the living room, blocking the arched doorway with my spread-eagled body. "You terrorized the horses and made a mess in the paddock!"

"Scoop, ain't you a might hard on the boy?" Dotty coaxed.

But she wasn't going to get my brother out of this one. "Plus, he left Grandad by himself *all* day. And when I got back, the whole kitchen was flooded!"

Quicker than a colt, B.C. slipped under my arm-blockade to the living room.

"Is Jared okay?" Dotty asked before I could chase my brother.

"Grandad? As okay as he ever is, I guess," I said. Dotty didn't say anything, but I still felt bad. Getting Alzheimer's disease wasn't Grandad's idea. "I'm sorry, Dotty, but it's not fair. I have to do everything, and B.C. gets away with murder."

Dotty listened quietly while I dramatized the flood account, ratted out B.C., and griped about Mrs. Buckingham, Stephen, and his girlfriend, Ursula.

With plastic grocery bags still dangling from each arm, Dotty smiled at me. "You're a good girl, Scoop. We'll just have to trust the good Lord with your grandaddy and everything else." She dropped her bags on the kitchen table.

"My verses," she said, picking up one of the slips of paper I'd set out to dry.

"Your what?"

"Memory verses." Dotty squinted at the faded writing. "Hope I can remember them. I think this one here was from Romans 3—verse 11, I believe. I been keeping some by the sink so's I could say 'em over while I do dishes." She dug other wads of paper from her apron pocket.

"These here I got for when things get slow down at the Hy-Klas."

Dotty reached up to put away a can of beans in the top cupboard. Her hand flew to her back, and she winced. "Can't say things slowed down much today though. Mr. Ford oughta be happy."

She took out two Styrofoam containers and a plastic plate of something rust-colored on noodles. Dinner. "I'd best check on your grandad. Set the table, will ya, Scoop?"

"Dotty, did you forget about my Horsefeathers meeting at 7:00?" A wave of self-pity washed over me like gray paint. "I told you about it this morning. And I've got to work Cheyenne again before the meeting."

Dotty sighed. "I must be getting old. You go on along and have fun."

Fun? She did not understand my life. I glanced at her half of a verse drying on the table: "no one who understands." *Amen to that!*

6

As always, Orphan heard me the second I set foot in the lane. It doesn't matter if I show up on foot, on my bike, or in a car. She knows it's me. She nickered and tossed her head to show off her long, black mane.

"Orphan!" I called, feeling full-force the miracle of belonging to her. She'd been the horse nobody wanted—especially not my grandad. I'd been the kid nobody wanted until my folks finally adopted me when I was 3. I'd nursed the coal-black orphan colt back to health, and she'd helped me back too.

Orphan stretched her neck over the fence. I sat on the top rail and let her rest her head in my lap.

"How's my best girl?" I scratched her ears until her eyelids drooped. "You know I'd rather ride you than anything. But the Zuckers are paying us to tame that wild Paint of theirs. Have you gotten Cheyenne good and worn out for me?"

Orphan sighed from deep in her chest. It was

great when she and Cheyenne ran together in the pasture and the Paint burned off some of her orneriness.

I tore myself away from my horse and walked out to meet Cheyenne. The mare still didn't come every time I called her, but at least she never ran from me.

It didn't take long to brush Cheyenne and saddle her Western. Orphan and I never ride with the saddle. I love the feel of her when I'm bareback. But I was training Cheyenne for Jen to ride, and she would be riding Western.

Jen Zucker, a great rider herself, just hadn't spent enough time around horses to pick up horse sense, to know what they're thinking. And with Cheyenne, you needed to know what she was thinking about doing next so you could out-guess her. For the Zuckers, a family with nine kids, I guess Cheyenne wasn't the ideal horse. But she was a good-natured sweetheart, and I was grateful Mr. Zucker hadn't sold her. Only I was pretty sure the Zuckers *would* sell her if I couldn't get her rough edges smoothed out.

I pulled on the protective riding hat just in case. Cheyenne had tried to throw me the first week we had her at Horsefeathers. I figured she still might give it a try just for fun, if she had the chance. I wouldn't give her the chance.

Cheyenne and I rode through all her paces in a shortened circle, using the dry side of the paddock. She liked to tighten and bunch up, arching her neck until her chin touched her chest. It looked beautiful, but kept the power with her and wore out the rider. I'd been throwing her off guard by loosening the rein when she slowed even a little bit. When I sensed she was about to speed up, I reined her in, but slacked off as soon as I could.

It was working. This second workout proved better than the first.

"I see you're using the Monty Montana method of reining." Jen Zucker stuck her head out of the barn and leaned against the doorpost.

"Am I?" I called. Jen reads so much that she knows more about what I'm doing with the horses than I do.

"She looks good, Scoop. I think Cheyenne likes the lighter bit."

"You're right," I said, eager to talk about the training with someone, especially Jen. "I moved to the littlest broken bit she'd—"

"Hey! There's Maggie *Peach*, by the look of her." Jen ran toward Maggie and Moby, who were walking up the lane. Maggie's totally peach outfit—even her hair had a peach streak—matched Moby's saddle blanket.

Jen is as fair-skinned as Maggie is dark. All the Zucker kids have blond hair and light skin. Maggie looked as happy to see Jen as Jen was to see her.

48

They talked a mile a minute while I finished cooling Cheyenne. I wanted to quit while we were ahead and she was acting nice. Jen helped me brush her and turn her out. Maggie did the same with Moby.

"Where did the mud come from?" Maggie asked. The puddles had soaked into the earth, but the paddock was still a muddy mess. "Long story, Maggie," I said. "The short answer is B.C."

"Where's Carla?" Jen asked, as the three horses trotted off together, keeping their distance from Ham.

"Don't know," I said, hanging up the lead rope. "She's usually here before Maggie."

"Spring is usually here before Maggie," Jen teased.

"I heard that," Maggie said. "You know," she said slowly, picking up a stick and making a line in the dirt, "I have a theory about Carla—why she's been so nervous lately."

"This should be good," Jen said. "Another Maggie Theory."

Maggie kept doodling in the dirt with the stick, making a big *3*, then a *7*. *Thirty-seven.* "I don't want to repeat gossip, *but* my mom heard that the Buckinghams are getting a divorce."

"Horsefeathers, Maggie!" I cried. "You're kidding!"

Maggie shrugged. "Just a rumor—but didn't you say you knew something was up with Carla, that she was worried about something?"

"Yeah," I admitted. "I just meant that Carla's been nervous or uptight about *something*. I mean, I know that's why Ham's gotten so spooked lately. He senses something's wrong. But I didn't mean this. A divorce? Are you sure, Maggie?"

Maggie shrugged her knowing shrug and tossed the stick to the grass. "No, I'm not sure. It's just something my mom heard. But it makes sense, Scoop. You have to admit."

It made more sense than Maggie knew. I hadn't told anybody about the argument I'd overheard at Buckingham Palace. "I hope you're wrong, Maggie."

"So do I," Jen said. "It would be awful to go through a divorce."

"You're telling me?" Maggie asked. "You're looking at the survivor of three divorces."

Nobody said anything for a couple of seconds. Then Jen glanced at her watch. "Come on," she commanded. "We still need to meet. And we can't wait for Carla any longer. We'll have to start without her. I promised Mom I'd get back as soon as I could to help put the triplets to sleep. I've been reading *Pilgrim's Progress* to them."

"That should do it all right," Maggie said, as we trailed to the barn. "Now, if Travis wants someone to read to him, give me a call." She batted her long eyelashes.

The triplets are just over 6 months old. Travis is 16 and makes you think of a muscular Palomino stallion.

We headed for Grandad's office, which we'd turned into a Horsefeathers meeting room. The floors and walls are wood, and the room has an old leather smell. Jen keeps our books and balances the checkbook. She had taken over the desk that filled half of the room. I wasn't complaining. Jen's a whiz with business and money and stuff. I have all I can handle with the horses.

Jen eased into the swivel chair. It creaked as she settled in. Maggie hopped up on the desk. "Nice threads, by the way, Scoop," Maggie said, grinning.

I stuck out my tongue at her. "Some of us work for a living, you know, Miss Peach." Actually I'd meant to change at home, but I didn't get around to it. I was still wearing my torn, muddy shirt, and jeans that were damp from the knees down due to the kitchen flood. Dotty hadn't even noticed.

"Still," Jen said seriously, "what if a potential boarder showed up, Scoop? What if they came to look us over and saw you like that?" Jen eyed me up and down. "You're a stable manager now. You have to think of these things. How *did* you get like that anyway?"

Maggie answered before I could. "I'll bet it has something to do with the muddy paddock, right?" I nodded. "And I'll bet the muddy paddock has something to do with your little brother."

"Right again," I said, feeling my anger at B.C. bubble to the surface again. I stepped backwards and bumped into an old sawhorse in the back corner of the office. Grandad had left a Western saddle on it. The heavy, dark brown saddle looked rotten, but the leather was too dirty to tell. I pulled down saddle soap and a sponge.

"Scoop," Jen scolded. "What are you doing?"

"Just a sec," I said. I grabbed a coffee can off the shelf and ran outside to fill it with water.

Jen glared at me when I came back in and set to work on the old saddle. "Go on," I said, ignoring Jen's scowl. "I'm listening. Honest."

"Good," Jen said. "Because we have serious matters to consider, Scoop. I'm not kidding around here."

Something in Jen's tone made my stomach hurt. Maggie got quiet too.

"I've been going over our finances," Jen said. Her steel blue eyes aimed over her wire-rimmed glasses, like Clark Kent shooting out X-ray vision. I couldn't have looked away if I'd wanted to.

"What, Jen? Go ahead! What's wrong?" Maggie asked, since I couldn't get the words out.

Jen shook her head. "There's no way around it. Horsefeathers Stable has serious money troubles."

7

The three of us sat still as dust in the Horse-feathers office. A pressure behind my eyes made my head ache. I'd almost lost everything a few weeks earlier. These past two weeks, watching the barn transform into a home for backyard horses, had been a miracle. I hadn't gotten over being thankful for it. And now we might lose the whole thing again?

"Horsefeathers, Jen! We paid Grandad's mortgage," I said. "We can't be broke!"

"That is accurate," Jen said, opening the green record-keeping book in front of her. "That payment takes us through the end of the month. So we should be okay with the bank for another two weeks."

Okay then. We should be okay. I tried to hold onto those words. I tried to pray.

"What about horse feed?" Maggie asked dramatically, as if rehearsing a scene from *Gone with the Wind*. "Will our babies starve?"

Jen sighed. "They won't starve, Miss Maggie Scarlet. I've budgeted the feed."

"Then we're okay, right?" I asked, dipping the sponge in water and rubbing hard at the tin of saddle soap. *Dear God*, I prayed, *please let it be okay.* I exhaled, suddenly aware that I'd been holding my breath. "You almost gave me a heart attack, Jen."

"We have to think about next month, and the months after that," Jen explained. "This is a business. And we are in bad shape financially. We need new boarders."

"No sweat!" Maggie said, standing up on the desk and extending her arms as if speaking to the masses. "Once the world discovers Scoop, The Teen Horse Whisperer, they'll be galloping to Horsefeathers in herds!"

"For now," Jen said, ignoring Maggie and still looking serious, "let's just be sure we keep the clients we have. Success is our best advertisement."

"That's not going to be so easy," I said. "Orphan and I kinda ran into Mrs. Buckingham this morning." In my mind I could picture Mrs. Buckingham, anger flashing from her eyes, her mouth in a tight, straight line. "She's only giving us to the end of the month to get Ham straightened out. She thinks it's my fault that her horse is so jumpy, Horsefeathers' fault."

"Then Stephen Dalton and that horrible Hurl-Something girl were telling the truth?" Maggie asked, doing ballet exercises while she talked. "They really had been talking to Mrs. Buckingham?"

"Hurl-Something?" Jen repeated. "Who's the Hurl-Something girl?"

"Ursula," I explained. "She's Stephen's new girlfriend."

"Ick," Jen said. "Stephen Dalton has a girlfriend? What's wrong with her?"

"I can't believe I forgot to tell you about her," Maggie said. "We met them. It was really sick."

"Ursula boards her horse at Dalton Stables," I said. "She and Stephen hung around here this morning and caught Ham and Moby fighting."

"Moby did not fight!" Maggie protested. "Moby was an innocent victim."

"Anyway," I continued, "Stephen made sure we knew that Mrs. Buckingham had dropped by Dalton Stables looking for an open stall. Maggie and I hoped they were just saying it to make me crazy."

"This is awful!" Jen exclaimed. "We can't afford to lose that monthly boarding fee, Scoop."

"I think it would be worse to have Scoop's reputation sullied!" Maggie exclaimed.

"Sullied?" I asked.

"You know," Maggie explained. "Dirtied. Tarnished. Destroyed—as in you couldn't keep a great horse so why should anybody trust you with a troubled horse, as in—"

"I get the picture, Maggie," I said.

Jen sat up straight in the desk chair and folded her hands on the desk. "I wish Carla would get here. Maybe she'd know how we can win over her mother. We have to hold on to that horse."

I knew we needed that boarding fee. And I could understand how losing Buckingham's business might damage Horsefeathers' reputation. But those weren't the only reasons I didn't want Ham to go to Dalton Stables. I'd come to care a lot about Carla's horse, and I didn't want to see him cooped up 21 hours a day in a boring stall. At Dalton Stables a horse definitely can't be a horse. No rolling in the mud, no free runs in the pasture, no rides through ponds.

"—Carla's with Ray." Maggie was saying something, but I'd missed it.

"What did you say, Maggie?" I asked.

"I just said Carla might be out with Ray. Maybe they ... forgot time." She said it in a dreamy, romantic voice.

"What are you talking about, Maggie?" I asked.

"Carla and Ray, Scoop," she said, twisting a brown curly lock around her little finger. "Where've you been? They're going out."

I felt weird inside. I knew Ray liked Carla. But he'd been *my* friend first. In fact, he'd been my first friend. I'd known Ray Cravens for more than 11 years, since I was 3, the first week I was adopted. Carla, on the other hand, hadn't even lived in West Salem a month.

I peered out the office door and through the open stall to the pasture. *Horsefeathers.* Why should it matter to me if they were together or not? But the least Carla could do was show up for the Horsefeathers meeting.

The barn door slid back with a thud, and I heard running footsteps at the other end of the barn. "Scoop! Maggie! Jen! Where are you?"

Maggie hollered out the office door, "Carla? We're in here!" To Jen and me, she whispered, "I've never heard Carla shout so loud. Frankly, I'm glad to hear she can."

"Scoop?" Carla's voice and footsteps drew closer as I continued to stare out the window. "Wait till you hear!"

Carla, gasping for breath, burst into the office. Her black hair, always perfectly styled, looked as wild as mine. Sweat made her white Polo shirt stick to her. And she hadn't tucked it into her riding breeches. Something really *was* wrong. I pushed Ray out of my mind.

"What is it?" I asked, dropping the sponge and rushing to her. "Did something happen?"

Carla gasped and leaned on the desk. She tried to talk between breaths. " ... heard ... ta ... roo ... yellin' ... wait ... "

"What's she saying?" Jen asked, looking to me for help.

I couldn't understand it either. "Did you hear something, Carla?" The argument I'd overheard that morning at Buckingham Palace replayed in my head. Maybe there had been another blowup at her house. I hoped that wasn't it.

Carla started crying. She opened her mouth, but couldn't get anything out but sobs.

"What's the matter?" Maggie asked, tears forming at her eyes too. "Is it your mother?"

Carla nodded and buried her head in her hands.

Maggie and Jen and I exchanged glances, but nobody said anything. And the only sounds in the barn were Carla's sniffles and Ham's confused whinny drifting in from his lonely pasture.

8

Jen led Maggie to the desk chair. "Here, Carla," she said, taking charge. "Sit down. Hang your head low between your knees. Now, relax. Breathe in. Breathe out." Jen looked up and whispered to Maggie and me. "I just finished reading *Practical Medicine for the 21st Century*."

It worked. In a minute, Carla's breathing evened out. She lifted her head. On her face, instead of the raw agony I expected to see, was a smile as big as a horse's grin.

"Carla? What?" Maggie cried. "I can't stand it! Talk!"

"I was all ready to come to the Horsefeathers meeting," Carla explained. "I was sitting on my bed and pulling on boots when my parents started yelling at each other. Their bedroom is right next to mine."

"Carla," I said, "I'm sorry. You know adults never mean what they say to each other, not when they're mad. Nobody means stuff in an argument." Like I knew. Dotty never argued. And B.C. and I hadn't argued lately. We'd fought.

59

"No, listen," she said, still smiling. It was eerie. "Mother and Father argue all the time. It's no big deal. I started to take out my hearing aids. That's what I do when they fight." She grinned at us and tapped one hearing aid. "Too bad you guys can't do it. Shuts out all the bad."

"Cool," Maggie said. "I could have used that when Mom was married to Husband #2."

"Well," Carla continued, "I *started* to take out the hearing aids, but something I heard stopped me." She broke into that huge smile and shook her head, like she still couldn't get over it.

"What?" Jen asked. "What did you hear?"

Carla went on. "Mother said, 'This is going to change all of our lives—Carla's too!' Well, I've had enough change in the past year—not that moving here and being part of Horsefeathers hasn't been the best thing that's ever happened to me," she added quickly. "But I still wanted to be prepared. I cranked up the volume on my hearing aids and listened through the wall."

"And?" Maggie said, waving her hands like a conductor.

"This is how it went." Carla repeated her parents' conversation, using two different voices. It was a performance that would have done even Maggie proud.

"'You can't mean it!' Father yelled. 'How could this possibly happen? How could you let it happen?'

"'Me?' Mother screamed. 'I suppose it's all my fault! *You're* not the one who will be left in this rathole! How dare you blame me!'"

So far I didn't see anything to smile about. The argument wasn't much different from the one I'd overheard that morning.

Maggie's eyes widened, as if she were watching the drama unfold. Jen scowled, her eyebrows almost meeting above her tiny nose.

"'We can work this out,' Father said, a little calmer, quieter, so he wasn't as easy to hear. I missed some of it.

"'*We?*' Mother yelled, very easy to hear. '*I'm* the one who will be stuck here all day. Are *you* going to quit *your* job to stay home, Edward? ... I didn't think so!'"

Carla switched to her own voice. "I still had no idea what was going on. Until I barely heard Father say, 'How did you find out? How long have you known?'"

Maggie gasped. "He's having an affair!" She reached over the desk and squeezed Carla's hand. "*How did you find out? How long have you known?*" Maggie repeated. "That's exactly what Mom's Husband #2 said when she caught him!"

Carla shook her head. "No! That's not it, Maggie."

"Of course that's not it, Maggie," Jen said. "Go on, Carla."

Carla grinned. "It was when Mother answered him that I knew, that I understood." Carla mimicked her mom's voice again. "'I suppose I suspected for almost a month, Edward. This morning I did a test to be sure. I'm sure.'"

But the final news was too good for Carla to give us in her mother's voice. She reached out and hugged me, the closest one to her. She'd never hugged me before.

When she let go, she had tears again. "Mother is pregnant! I'm going to be a big sister!"

Seconds passed with no noise except Moby sneezing and another horse somewhere stamping in his stall.

"That's it?" Maggie asked.

"They're just having one baby?" Jen asked. She'd gone through twin and triplet Zucker babies. One baby was no news.

I saw Carla's smile collapse, so I forced a smile of my own. "Carla, that's great!" I said, trying to sound excited. "Really. I ... we ... know how much you've wanted a brother or sister."

Maggie got the idea too. "Yeah, that's great!" she said, sounding much more sincere than I did. Even I thought she meant it, until I remembered she's an actress.

Maggie bubbled now. "I've never really had a *real* sister or brother. I get steps. And there's not much you can do with them because somebody else has ruined them already. But yours will be different! You get to start from scratch. We'll dress your little sister up and teach her all about boys and horses, not in that order. She can call me Aunt Maggie!"

Jen wasn't buying Maggie's act. "Why not call you Aunt 37?"

Carla tugged on her pony tail. "I—I know it sounds silly to you guys. Especially to you, Jen. But my house has always been so lonely. It never felt like home in Lexington. And our house here ... well, it's nice and all. But it's not home either. Even with my hearing aids turned up all the way, it's too quiet."

The thought flashed through my mind and I wondered if the baby would have normal hearing. I wasn't about to ask Carla though. She was getting her grin back. At least now I knew Maggie's rumor was just that—a rumor. The Buckinghams wouldn't be having a baby if they planned on getting divorced.

"You know, Carla," I said, "now that you're into the brother and sister market, how about taking B.C. off my hands? I'd let you have him in a hoofbeat."

"Hey! Anybody home but us horses?" Ray Cravens poked his long, tanned neck into the office. Ray has long everything—arms, legs, feet. You'd think he'd be clumsy or gangly, but he's as smooth and easygoing as a Tennessee Walking

Horse. Plus, he's just about the only boy I don't get tongue-tied around.

"Sorry, Ray," Jen said. "This is an official Horsefeathers meeting."

I grinned at him. "And we just elected *you* Chief Mucker, in charge of mucking all stalls. Congratulations!"

Ray grinned back, the only person I know who can give you a wide grin without showing teeth. His eyes smile. "Well, thank you, Miss Scoop. I'm honored." But I saw those eyes dart around. Searching for a glimpse of Carla?

Carla raced over to Ray and gripped his forearm with both hands to pull him into the office. But she didn't let go once he was in. It was such a natural holding on that it made me think Maggie had been right. Maybe they *were* going out. I had to look away.

"Ray!" Carla said, almost whispering in his ear, for crying out loud. "I'm going to be a sister!"

"A nun?" Ray asked, the grin wiped totally from his face.

We burst into laughter, and the tension that maybe only I felt, relaxed.

"Not *that* kind of sister, you dummy!" Maggie said, still laughing hard.

Carla took a deep breath. "Ray, Mother's pregnant!"

"Cool," Ray said. His voice always sounds the same, so I couldn't tell what he really thought about Carla's news. I think he was still feeling grateful that Carla hadn't decided to become a nun.

Carla had just started filling Ray in on her parents' big argument, when a blast of clanging and blaring erupted like a bomb over our heads.

Ray covered his ears and mouthed, "What is it?"

"B.C.!" I screamed. But my cry was drowned out by the pounding and screeching coming from the roof.

I raced outside and ran to the middle of the paddock, where I could see B.C.'s favorite part of the roof. I almost slipped in the mud again, but caught myself before I went down.

My little brother was standing up on top of the barn, juggling bottle caps, while his music blared. The sun hung low behind him, ready to drop behind the barn. Its reddish glow made B.C. look like an evil shadow, a sinister, sizzling weather vane.

"Turn it off, B.C!" I screamed as loud as I could.

He kept juggling, pretending not to notice me.

I searched for something to throw at him to make him look at me. Mud slurped at my boots everywhere I stepped. Someone was singing— more like yelling—from B.C.'s boom box. I reached down and picked up an old corn cob half buried in the mud.

At the barn door Maggie and Jen were waving at me, trying to get my attention, motioning for me to stop. They must have thought I was going to hurt B.C.

"It's okay!" I yelled, muddy corn cob in hand. "I won't hit him."

With a firm grasp on the cob, I hauled back to get a good throw. Only my arm bumped into something. It threw me off balance. I wobbled and fell backwards, pushing something down with me.

Or someone.

"Help!" screamed a voice behind me, right in my ear, as we splatted in the mud, me on top.

"Get off of me!" someone yelled.

I knew that yell. I rolled over and struggled to my feet.

There, sitting flat in the muddy paddock at my boots was Carla Buckingham's mother.

9

Carla sloshed through the mud toward us, while I just stood staring down at her mud-covered mother. Mrs. Buckingham's green business suit was caked in mud. She shook globs of slime off her arm, splattering me. Her neat, black hair, still half in a stylish twist, looked like it had been frosted with chocolate icing.

"Mother, are you all right?" Carla asked. She helped her to her feet and retrieved a green high heel from the mud. "Are you sure you're okay?" Carla was fawning over her as if she were made of glass.

Then I remembered. Mrs. Buckingham was pregnant.

"Horsefeathers," I said. "I'm so sorry! I didn't see you! I didn't mean to—"

She stepped back. "Stay away from me!"

Carla moved between us, like she had to protect her mother from me. "It's okay, Mother," she said. "Scoop was just trying to get B.C.'s attention."

Maggie, Ray, and Jen had come out to the paddock, but stopped where the mud started.

"I like your suit!" Maggie called over.

The music had stopped, but I couldn't remember it shutting off. B.C. was nowhere in sight. Lucky for him. I could have creamed him! Of all people to knock into the mud, why did it have to be Mrs. Buckingham, the very client I was supposed to be bending over backwards to keep happy?

Well, we'd sure bent over backwards. But she didn't look happy.

"Welcome to Horsefeathers?" I said, my voice cracking on *feathers* so I sounded like Grandad, who'd given me the word *horsefeathers* in the first place. I cleared my throat when Mrs. Buckingham didn't answer.

"Why *did* you come to Horsefeathers, Mother?" Carla asked. "And are you positive you feel okay? You didn't fall too hard? I guess it's a good thing the ground is so muddy or you might have been really hurt." Carla picked mud out of her mother's collar as she rambled.

Mrs. Buckingham brushed her away. "Quit fussing, Carla! I came to take you shopping in Kennsington. And I thought it might be a good opportunity to observe how Buckingham's British Pride is being handled at this ... this stable."

"We'll be glad to show you—" I said.

She stopped me cold. "I've seen quite enough," she said. She pointed to the corner of the paddock, where Ham stood by himself, watching the whole thing from his pasture. By the looks of him, the horse had at least learned something at Horsefeathers Stable. He'd learned how to roll in the mud. He was as caked with mud as Mrs. Buckingham and I were. It made him look more like a dapple gray than a champion bay.

"That horse has never been so disgustingly filthy! The grooms here are incompetent!" Mrs. Buckingham exclaimed, apparently unaware that "the grooms" were me.

"That's not true!" Maggie said, tiptoeing closer. "Scoop brushes each horse twice a day, and sometimes more. Ham—Bucking-ham's Whatever—needs to roll in the mud *more*!"

Carla held up her hand—crossing guard style—to stop Maggie's speech. "You see, Mother," she explained, "the mud cakes onto the horses' hairs. Then when they roll, dead hairs come off. It's more efficient than brushing. But we do that too, of course," she added quickly. "My horse still can't quite roll all the way over, not all the time. But Scoop says once he relaxes and gets used to the freedom of running in pastures and playing with the other horses, he'll be able to roll over several times at once, just like Orphan."

"Like Orphan?" Mrs. Buckingham said it like a swear word. "That's the goal here? To make the horses like *Orphan*? That's what you want for your purebred American Saddle Horse? To behave like a mongrel, mixed breed?"

A hot lump rose through my throat. I was glad Orphan couldn't understand her.

Carla glanced at me like a frightened rabbit. "Mother, listen, please! Scoop says—"

"Scoop says? Scoop says!" Mrs. Buckingham spoke in a controlled voice, inches from Carla's nose, while the rest of us studied our shoes. "Don't you dare quote a little teenager to me! I let you keep your horse here against my better judgment. But this is too much. Since Buckingham's British Pride has been in this stable, he has lost ground. He's nervous and filthy, and he's losing his competitive edge. Do you hear me, young lady?"

Zuckers' goats could have heard her from the other end of town.

Jen had been hanging back, but now she spoke up. "Mrs. Buckingham, if I may interject with an objective evaluation, your horse is actually working smoother now than before he came to Horsefeathers. He's moving out more willingly, a trait that will pay off in the long run. He *is* a little nervous, but Carla never has to use the crop now."

Thank you, Jen! I knew those few words weren't easy for Jen, who likes to stay out of arguments. And she was right. Carla hadn't used the little leather whip since day two at Horsefeathers.

Mrs. Buckingham narrowed her eyes at Jen, then shot a glare at me. "I know that I said I'd give you until the end of the month with this horse. I'll pay you what I owe you, but I just don't know if I can leave the horse here another two weeks."

She turned to Carla. "They have a stall opening up next Tuesday at Dalton Stables, Carla. I've spoken to Ralph Dalton about booking Buckingham's British Pride there next month. But I firmly believe we should move as soon as they can take us."

She stood up straight, looking as poised as if she weren't covered in mud. "Besides, at Dalton Stables they have stable shows the last day of each month. It's just for the boarded horses, to keep them sharp and competitive. So if we're there before the end of the month, our horse can perform in the Dalton Show."

"But then he'll miss the Horsefeathers Show," Maggie said. She said it like she didn't really care one way or the other. She said it like we were actually having a Horsefeathers Show.

Maggie's lips formed a straight line as she cocked her head at Mrs. Buckingham and shrugged a silent *too bad for you, though*.

I opened my mouth to say something, but Ray elbowed me in the side.

Maggie, all sweetness and honey now, reached out to Carla's mom and shook her hand. "Mrs. Buckingham, I can't say what a pleasure it is to meet you at last. I've heard so-o-o much about you!" Maggie's accent had transformed into her Northeastern Bostonian aristocracy accent.

"I don't believe we have ev-ah met, officially that is. Maggie 37 Peach. I too board my horse here at the Horsefeathers Establishment. It's a shame you'll miss the show."

Mrs. Buckingham looked confused for half a second. Then she recovered. "Yes, I'm sure that's fine for you, but—"

"Tuesday. The show is Tuesday. I heard your horse was to be featured in some way?" Maggie looked toward Carla, perplexed.

"Carla," said her mother, "you didn't tell me anything about a show."

Duh! I thought. How about she hasn't said anything because there isn't going to be a show? I gave Maggie my cross-eyed look, and she smiled sweetly back at me. I wanted to choke her.

Carla's eyes got huge. Then she faked a smile and shrugged.

Maggie took over. "Carla probably didn't want to ruin the surprise. Listen, I have an idea. You probably can't move into Dumpton Stables—"

"*Dalton* Stables," Mrs. Buckingham corrected.

"Yes, *Dilton* Stables," Maggie continued, "until after Tuesday, true?"

"I suppose that's true," conceded Mrs. Buckingham.

"So it sounds as if you'll be here for our show anyway. Why not come to the Horsefeathers

Show and see for yourself how your horse performs? The event promises to be amazing. You won't be disappointed."

"I do like the idea of a show here," she said slowly, as if talking to herself. "It might even give us an edge for the Dalton Show—not that we need an edge, of course."

"Of course," Maggie agreed.

Mrs. Buckingham looked back at Carla. "All right. We'll stay for the show."

"Great!" Carla said. "And you'll see how great my horse is doing at Horsefeathers, Mother."

"I didn't say we're keeping him here," said her mother. "Let's just wait and see what happens Tuesday."

"Lovely," said Maggie.

We watched Carla and her mother walk away into the darkening night.

"Maggie 37 Peach," I whispered, "what have you gotten us into now?"

10

I don't get it!" Carla muttered for the thousandth time. She heaved the saddle off Ham. The bay jerked at the cross-ties, but Carla didn't seem to notice. "When are they going to break the big news?"

"Easy," I said to Ham. But I wanted to say it to Carla. It was Thursday already. On Tuesday we'd be putting on Horsefeathers Horse Show for the sole purpose of showing how well Ham was doing. But with Carla still so wound up, Ham was acting more skittish than ever. I had cut our ride short because I didn't want to put him through any more misery or mixed signals.

"I just can't believe my parents haven't told me Mother is pregnant!" Carla jerked the saddle blanket off so suddenly Ham scooted sideways. "Why would they keep the baby a secret? What are they waiting for?"

I took the saddle and blanket from her and carried them to the tack room. I was beat. Ever since Maggie had come up with the idea of Horsefeathers Horse Show, she'd been tied up with acting rehearsals or piano lessons. I'd put in extra workouts on all the horses. Carla meant well, but she was doing Ham more harm than good. And she wasn't doing me much good either. On and on she yakked about all the things she wanted to do with her new brother or sister.

"Maybe they're waiting until the pregnancy shows," Carla suggested as I handed her a brush. "Either way, I don't think I can last much longer, Scoop. When do you think she'll *look* pregnant? No way can I wait *that* long!"

Carla didn't seem to notice that I'd stopped plugging into her conversation an hour ago—which was fine with me. I'm not big on talk. I brushed Ham on the opposite side and felt him quiver when the brush touched him. The least movement set him off.

"On the other hand," Carla was saying, "I do want *them* to be the ones who give me the big news." I heard her brush sweep Ham's mane.

"No chance they'll spill any news tonight though," she said. "Father is out of town as usual, and Mother's dining in the city with an old schoolmate or something. I *hate* eating alone, don't you?"

"I don't know," I said. "Dotty always makes B.C. and me sit down and eat together when she gets home from the Hy-Klas. Eating by myself sounds pretty good to me."

"Just think, Scoop," Carla said, as if she hadn't heard me. "Pretty soon I'll have a little sister or brother. I won't ever have to eat alone."

I sighed. God must have had His Spirit talking to me so loud I couldn't ignore it. I knew I should invite Carla home to supper with me, but I didn't want to. Carla had never been inside my house. The Buckinghams probably ate with silver spoons on bone china—whatever that is.

"Done," Carla said, patting Ham. "I guess I might as well head home."

"Wait a minute," I said. "Dotty would kill me if she found out I let you go home for supper alone. Come eat with us."

"Oh, I couldn't do that, Scoop," Carla said.

"Why not?" I asked coldly. It was one thing for *me* to feel like my house and supper weren't good enough for her. It was another thing if *she* felt that way.

"I couldn't impose on your aunt, Scoop. She may not have enough prepared. My mother goes nuts if Father brings home one of his business partners with less than a two-week warning."

I laughed as I untied Ham and led him to his stall. "Enough *prepared*? No problem. Dotty doesn't prepare."

We watched the bay as he marched straight through his stall and outside. Orphan and Moby didn't even bother to lift their heads from grazing. The late afternoon sun burned as bright as

76

noon. Grasshoppers popped up all around like Mexican jumping beans. Their landings on dried ground sounded like fire crackling.

"Carla Buckingham," I said, "get ready for an eating experience at the Coop Family Funny Farm. I just hope for your sake you're not really hungry."

Carla protested most of the walk home, but she came with me.

"Dotty! We're home!" I cried, taking Carla through the front door just in case floods had struck again in the kitchen.

"It's nice, Scoop," Carla said. "It's so homey."

I glanced at Dotty's scratchy, gold couch and Grandad's vinyl, green recliner, complete with a six-inch strip of wide gray tape on the seat to keep the stuffing in. The rest of the living room looked more like an attic. The house had a wet, musty smell mixed with odor of what I'd come to think of as old age. If Carla had been expecting to smell supper on the stove, she was already disappointed.

"Homey," I muttered, switching on the small lamp closest to the door. It was a porcelain dog's head, and the nose held a light switch chain. "Right." Yellowed window shades hung at half-mast. Sunlight stirred up white lines of dust, slanted stripes pointing down to the brown-gold shag carpet.

Dotty yelled from B.C.'s old room, "Scoop? That you? Give us a hand here, will ya? I can't get Grandad—" Each word was punctuated with a grunt. Then she broke off.

I shot Carla a weak smile and headed for the room that used to be a laundry room before we made it over for my brother. Then Grandad took it over when his Alzheimer's disease made him so he couldn't live by himself.

"Dotty, I brought—"

I didn't finish. Grandad was sitting on his bed, clutching a wastebasket. His chin stretched out over the top of the plastic white bin. "You can't have them neither!" he barked, sneering at me. "Blamed females!"

The tiny room was twice as long as it was wide, with Grandad's bed and dresser taking up the whole length of one wall. The three of us barely fit. The air smelled like baby powder and iodine.

I heard Carla at the doorway and glanced back at her. "Sorry," I said.

She shook her head and nodded for me to help Grandad.

"Hey, Grandad," I said. "I just got back from the barn. Orphan sends you her greetings."

"Half-breed horse," he muttered. "Horsefeathers! How am I supposed to run a horse farm of purebreds when that blamed horse is there? You want my things for that there horse, I betcha."

I wanted to tell him that Orphan is 100 times better than any of the purebreds he used to sell. I wanted to tell him that he didn't have a farm anymore. Horsefeathers was *my* responsibility now. I wanted to tell him to go stuff himself in his wastebasket.

I closed my eyes and apologized to God for thinking mean things. Then I thanked Him for at least helping me not say them out loud.

"Nice wastebasket, Grandad," I said.

"Jared Coop," Dotty said, sounding worn out. "You're being silly, and you know it. Now, you can't go throwing away all them spoons! What would you eat your chocolate pudding with?"

Grandad gritted his teeth and hugged his wastebasket tighter. I'd told Dotty she shouldn't give him a wastebasket. Already he'd dumped sugar and flour in it. And before that, he hid our mail there.

Suddenly B.C. was in the room. He plopped down next to Grandad as if his grandfather didn't have a wastebasket in his lap.

"Grandad," B.C. said, "want to play catch with a bottle cap?"

And just like that, Grandad stood up, put the wastebasket back in exactly the right place behind the door, and followed B.C. out.

As soon as Grandad was out of sight, I fished spoons out of the wastebasket. Carla stooped down to help.

"Dotty," I said, picking out a lone fork, "Carla's folks are gone. I knew you wouldn't want her to eat alone."

"I apologize, Ms. Coop," Carla said. "I know it's short notice."

"Now ain't you a polite and pretty little thing. Call me Dotty," she said, pointing to the plastic nametag she pinned on every day to work at the Hy-Klas.

I had a feeling Dotty wouldn't have any trouble understanding Carla's speech. Dotty had been kneeling on the floor, and now she used the bed to help her stand up, which looked like no easy task. "You could eat with us *every* night, Carla," she said. "Always room for one more."

Dotty sat on the edge of the bed. Her black pants hiked up, revealing short stockings that were probably supposed to go over her calf to her knee. On Dotty, the tan stockings quit just above her ankles, so her calfs bulged out. I wanted to hike her stockings up for her. And maybe shine the scuffed black shoes Maggie called sensible.

"That's really nice of you, Ms. Coop, Ma'am," Carla said.

"Not *Ma'am*, please!" Dotty begged, laughing. "Makes me sound like an old woman. I don't even let Scoop here call me Aunt. Dotty's good enough, I reckon."

"Sorry," Carla said, " ... Dotty."

80

Dotty stood up and slapped her right leg, like it might have gone to sleep. "Don't be sorry. Oh, and just for the records, it ain't Coop. Scoop's ma and me, we was sisters. So the name's still the one I was borned with. Dorothea Eberhart."

"I didn't know your first name was really Dorothea," I said, pulling another spoon out of the wastebasket.

Dotty scruffed my head on her way out. "I reckon there's a few things you might not know about me. Carla, glad to have you, Honey. Scoop, you girls wash. I'll get supper on." I heard her chuckling on her way to the kitchen.

"She's amazing!" Carla whispered as she double-checked the wastebasket and came up with a fork I'd missed. "How does she work all day and still get dinner at night?"

I grinned. "You're about to find out."

I was giving Carla the two-minute tour of my attic room—my horse statues, horse magazines, horse pillow—when Dotty hollered up at us. "Supper!"

I wondered if Carla had ever eaten "supper," or if all the evening meals at Buckingham Palace were dinners.

The five of us took our places. Grandad and B.C. sat at opposite ends of the table. Grandad got a real chair, like Carla. B.C. got the little step ladder. Dotty used the folding chair. And I sat on an old milking stool—so I could talk directly to their belly buttons.

I tried to read Carla's reactions to everything. She cracked her knuckles and drummed her fingers on the side of her chair. She seemed confused as she stared at the six or seven white Styrofoam containers in the center of the table. Some had names on top—*Pistachio*, *Waldorf*, *P.S.* for potato salad. Others just had prices scribbled in thick black marker: *$1.16, $2.43*. White tags glued to the sides or tops carried the juicy details in black type, plus the date—today's date—as the last possible day you should eat them.

Dotty handed each of us a spoon to go with the knife and fork on our napkins. Mine still felt wet, and I dried it on the napkin. Grandad grabbed his spoon before it touched paper. Our plates came from two different sets, both earned from Hy-Klas collection runs.

Dotty closed her eyes and took B.C. and Grandad's hands. I was between B.C. and Carla, so I took their hands. Carla reached over and let Grandad take her hand. Brave girl, I thought.

"Lord above," Dotty prayed, "it's good to be home." Nobody prays like Dotty, so natural you want to peek to make sure Jesus hasn't slipped in and sat down at the table while you had your eyes shut.

"Thank You, our Father, for another one of Your handmade, hand-picked days! You're just the best Father a family could have. We especially like how You're sharing Carla with us tonight. So thank You for providing this here food and friend. Make us as thankful as we are hungry. Amen."

I peeked a couple of times during Dotty's conversation with God. Carla was wide-eyed and staring at Dotty.

I tried not to worry about what Carla was thinking, but I couldn't help it. We probably looked like the Flintstones to her—or the Four Stooges.

"Come on, now," Dotty coaxed. "Don't be shy, Carla Honey. Not in this house. You like barbecue, Hon? Hy-Klas run a special all week on it. Lou cut up too much beef. Here." She dumped a huge helping onto Carla's plate.

"My mother doesn't shop," Carla said, pushing at the reddish brown glob on her plate. "Do you know Ruth Bowen? She comes in to clean three times a week. I think she gets our groceries in Kennsington."

"Well that makes it real nice, don't it?" Dotty said, dropping a glob of beef on Grandad's plate. "Don't tell Mr. Ford I says so, but things can get a bit pricey at the Hy-Klas. Them big stores sell enough to run discounts. Here, try the macaroni. I'm not much for pistachio pudding, but B.C. here likes it, dontcha, B.C.?"

B.C. didn't answer. He just kept chewing—with his mouth open so we could all see how much he likes barbecue.

Carla took her first bite. I wasn't the only one watching her. "Mmmm. You know, Mrs. Reguiero used to serve a dish that tasted just like this. She was our cook in Kentucky."

Once Carla took that first bite, she kept going. She tried every single container and went back to most for seconds.

"This is all so good!" Carla declared. "I don't usually eat this much. Maybe it's the company."

"Then you'll have to come home regular

with Scoop. We'll fatten you up. Is there just you and your folks in that big house?"

Carla wiped her mouth with the thin napkin with pictures of cows all over it. She glanced at me, then broke into a huge smile. "For now."

Dotty raised her bushy eyebrows above the rims of her glasses.

Carla set down her fork. "I guess it won't hurt to tell you if you *promise* not to tell anyone." Without waiting for Dotty's promise, she blurted out, "Mother's going to have a baby!"

Dotty gasped as if an honest-to-goodness bomb had just dropped into the pistachio pudding. "Well thank You, Jesus!" she said, glancing at the ceiling or heaven. Her eyes teared up, and she dabbed them with her cow napkin. "You take real good care of your mama, hear?"

I thought I knew why Dotty was teary-eyed. She was probably thinking of her sister. My mom had lost two babies by the time she gave up and adopted me. Dotty still visited two white crosses in the baby graveyard at the cemetery. Every time I rode my bike out past there, fresh purple flowers stuck out of baby jars by each cross. Dotty told me once that when my mom got pregnant with B.C., she had to stay in bed for weeks. And when he was born, she almost died.

Carla must have thought she'd finally found someone who understood what a great thing this was to get a sister or brother. "I overheard Mother and Father discussing it," she explained. "Now I'm going crazy trying to pretend I don't know so they can be the ones to tell me. I just don't understand what's taking them so long!"

"They might be afraid you'll be jealous," Dotty said.

"Jealous?" Carla repeated, as if she'd never thought of that possibility.

"Sure. Scoop's mama was mighty worried how she'd take to a little brother. Lots of kids go through that. They're usually pretty excited at first, until they have time to think on it a spell. Then they start suspecting their mamas and daddies ain't got love enough to go around. I reckon your folks are thinking something like that, Honey."

"Did she?" B.C. asked. It was the first thing he'd said at the table, and we all turned to stare at him. B.C. has a habit of showing up late in conversations, adding his two cents to a discussion that ended several quarters back.

"What, B.C. Honey?" Dotty asked, filling Grandad's chipped, white coffee cup. "Did who, what?"

"Did Scoop take to me as a brother?" he asked in a voice a normal person would save for the thousandth time asking.

"Well of course she did!" Dotty said. "She'd never send back a gift God gave her!"

"Of course that was before I got to know you, B.C.," I said, still mad about the mess he'd gotten me into. If it hadn't been for B.C., the paddock wouldn't have been muddy, I wouldn't have run outside to turn off his racket, I wouldn't have shoved Mrs. Buckingham in the mud, and we wouldn't have had to waste our time on a stupid stable show to try to keep our customer.

"Scoop's just kidding, B.C.," Dotty said.

I glared at my brother and shook my head no. He stuck his tongue out at me.

Carla pushed herself away from the table and slumped in her seat. "I am *so* full! I don't think I could eat another bite."

"Pistachio pudding." It wasn't a question or a command. Grandad said it in the same tone he'd said everything during supper, and that wasn't much: "Reba Mae Coop," (his wife, the grandmother I'd never met); "spoons, spoons, silverware;" "eighty-seven back posts;" and "horsefeathers." All in all, not a bad night. At least Grandad hadn't accused Carla of stealing macaroni salad or anything.

"Good idea, Jared!" Dotty made it sound like Grandad had come up with a theory worthy of Einstein.

Carla ate every drop of her pudding and scraped the plastic cup clean. "I am so glad I came," she said. "You wouldn't believe how boring dinners are with just Mother and Father and me. And even that's rare. Most of the time it's just Mother and me. I can't wait until I have a brother or sister. Then it will seem like a real family dinner."

I made a face at B.C.

"Well, you just keep thinking like that, Hon," Dotty said. "Don't you let that jealousy bird nest in your head. You hear?"

"I hear, Dotty," Carla said, springing to her feet. "I'm going home. Who knows? Tonight just may be the night. If Father closed his business deal and Mother found a boutique she loves, they just might be in a talking mood."

Dotty hugged Carla, and they said good-bye as if they were long-lost relatives who would never see each other again. When I walked Carla halfway home, she seemed more calm than she'd been for a long time. I hoped it would last—for Ham's sake.

B.C. disappeared after supper, so when I got back, I had to clear the table myself.

"Carla's a sweet little thing," Dotty said, running scalding hot water into the sink and rolling up her sleeves. "Sure is nervous though, ain't she?"

I got a clean dish towel. "Yeah," I said. "And when Carla's nervous, so is her horse. I hope she gets everything ironed out with her folks. Ham's got to do well at this horse show we're putting on, Dotty. If he doesn't, he'll end up at Dalton Stables." And no matter what, I couldn't let that happen.

12

I caught a glimpse of Ray in the barn doorway as I tied the knot on Cheyenne's girth strap. "Is Carla with you?" I called. It was Saturday and I hadn't heard from Carla since Thursday night's supper.

"I wish," Ray said, strolling up. "She about bit my head off on the phone last night. I asked her if she'd talked to her folks about being a sister. She said it was none of my business."

I slipped the bridle on Cheyenne and remembered what Dotty had said about being jealous. "Maybe she's having second thoughts, Ray."

"About me?" Ray asked, scratching his head of thick, black hair.

"No, Stupid," I said, wondering what Carla had that could make this easygoing Tennessee Walking Horse turn flighty as a Five-gaited American Saddle Horse. "Second thoughts about her mom having a baby. Carla's been the center of attention for 14 years."

"But she was so psyched about the baby," Ray said.

"I know. Maybe that's not it. But when she didn't come to Horsefeathers yesterday to work Ham for this show, I called her. She wouldn't come to the phone. It started me thinking. Dotty says it's natural to wonder if your parents have enough love to go around."

"Makes sense, I guess," he admitted.

Cheyenne stamped the stall floor. "Besides," I explained, "Carla ate supper at our house Thursday night. She probably got a good dose of B.C. and decided siblings aren't such a good deal after all."

"B.C.'s okay," Ray said.

I unhooked the cross-ties and led the Paint out toward the paddock.

"Scoop," Ray called after me, "if Carla shows up, ask her to call me."

I stopped and turned back to him. "Okay. And if you talk to her first, tell her I'm desperate. Maggie has a ballet performance this weekend, and Jen can't leave the little Zuckers until Mrs. Zucker gets home from visiting her sister in Kennsington. So if Carla doesn't show up, I'll have to work Ham besides the others. And there's still the north stalls to clean and the arena to rake." I gave him my best begging look.

"All right," he said. "Pass the pitchfork."

~~~~~~~~~~~~~~~~~~~~~~~~~~~~~~~

Carla didn't show all day Saturday. That night as I prayed, I folded up my attic room in my mind, as I did every night. I stared out and imagined my tiny window sucking in the stars and moon. Then my A-framed bedroom became a mental picnic blanket as I folded in my dresser, my horse posters, the horsefeather Carla had given me. It was really a cuckoo feather her dad brought home from one of his trips. Cuckoo birds leave their babies with "adopted" parents. Then the baby cuckoos grow up as part of the new family. Carla gave me the feather twice. The second time was the day I took over Horsefeathers Stable to remind me that I'd found a place where I belonged. After mentally folding in the cuckoo feather, I imagined folding in my bed, and finally me.

As I unfolded the room, I prayed and gave God His stars back, then my dresser, bed, the horsefeather, and myself. I prayed for Ham and Carla and wondered if either of them had any idea what was really at stake in the Horsefeathers Horse Show. I thought about Dotty's memory verse: "There is no one who understands," and I fell asleep praying those words back to God. *Nobody understands, God. There is no one who understands.*

~~~~~~~~~~~~~~~~~~~~~~~~~~~~~~

Usually I love Sundays. I need Sundays. It's the only day I don't run the horses through their training routines. After church, if I can, I just ride. Just plain ride. Just Orphan and me. Or sometimes I don't even ride. Orphan and I just hang out.

But this Sunday nothing was coming easy. Dotty had the nursery, which left me to mind Grandad and B.C. in church.

"Now Jared," Dotty said, leaving us at the basement steps, "you relax and worship the good Lord, hear?" She had on a navy dress with white polka dots. Even the belt had polka dots. She'd worn it the last several Sundays, and I had a suspicion it was the only dress that still fit. I also thought the dress maybe was supposed to be straight. On Dotty it reminded me of a pillow case too small for the pillow. She'd pulled her hair back in two combs above her ears, but one comb had already broken loose and hung upside down.

Still, you'd have thought Dotty was the prom queen, the way she greeted everybody, and they greeted back. "Howdy, Mrs. Winslow," she hollered across half a dozen pews. "Mr. Snyder, if you don't look spiffy!"

The bone-thin Mr. Snyder looked a thousand years old, but he brightened at Dotty's compliment and lifted his hand in a frozen wave.

Dotty padded down the cement stairs to the basement, leaving me to herd B.C. and Grandad into our pew, third from the back on the left. I slid in between them, with Grandad on the inside in case he got a mind to wander during the service, and B.C. on my other side in case he felt like singing in the wrong spots.

Grandad stared at the church bulletin as if it were a murder mystery. B.C. would have said that Grandad wasn't "at home" this morning. More and more, Grandad's Alzheimer's was taking him somewhere else and leaving his body with us. He still came back and even yelled at me like his old self some days. But more and more, whenever I stared into his tiny, gray eyes, it felt as if I were looking through a telescope with the cap on both ends. Nothing came in or out.

B.C. had started reporting on Grandad like a weather forecaster. "Grandad's home today" meant Grandad was acting kind of normal and knew where he was.

This morning B.C. had announced over Frosty Flakes, "He's gone," which meant Grandad wasn't responding.

I looked around the church for Carla. I couldn't believe she hadn't even called in almost three days. And now with the show on Tuesday, we'd only have Monday to do any real practicing. I didn't care if she *was* having trouble with the idea of sharing her parents. Carla and Ham's part in the show was the most important, since it was her mother we had to impress. She should have been at Horsefeathers.

A dozen pews up from us, Stephen Dalton was making a rare appearance in church. Next to him sat Ursula, with Stephen's arm wrapped around her shoulder. Thank goodness they were far enough away so I didn't have to look at that.

The organ started playing, but still no Carla. The Zuckers showed up like a hurricane, swirling down the aisle to their pews, second and third from the front on the right-hand side. Jen looked straight ahead, her cheeks pink. I followed Travis' long strides down the aisle behind Jen. In his suit, he looked at least 18.

I tugged at the hem of my denim skirt, which had gotten too short for me overnight. B.C. had on clean blue jeans and a white shirt. His hair was slicked down to the side, the way Dotty likes it. He looked about as comfortable as a weaned colt.

"I'm going down front to sit with Tommy," B.C. said, heading for the Zucker pew.

"Don't!" I grabbed for him but missed. If he got in trouble, I'd get blamed. B.C. stepped over four or five Zuckers to get to Tommy, who didn't look all that thrilled to see him.

The organ music got louder, and I heard Grandad hum. I turned to shush him and spotted Carla Buckingham standing in the back of the church. At first I didn't recognize her. Her hair was pulled back, and she wore white shorts and sandals. For the first time since I'd known her, I was more dressed up than she was.

I waved and tried to get Carla's attention. She glanced around the sanctuary, but her gaze never landed on me. I'd have to catch her after church.

Grandad's hum grew louder. I started to tell him to stop, but he had a good hum going. It went right along with the organ music. Grandad's eyes softened and focused. His lips moved, and then his hands. They stayed a few inches off his lap and waved in and out like a symphony conductor. Even when the Bach or Beethoven music took a weird turn, it didn't lose Grandad. He hummed a perfect harmony.

Grandad was home. I wished Dotty could see it. He hadn't been home like this for days. "Horsefeathers! You're good, Grandad," I whispered.

"Do you hear it ... right here?" he said, grinning at me, showing yellow teeth I couldn't ever remember seeing. "He switches to 3/4 time so the violins can answer the bass. Now it turns, da, da, da ... dum, dum, dum.

He sounded like my old music teacher. "Grandad," I whispered, "how do you—"

"Shh-h-h!" he hissed. "You'll miss the arpeggio."

The hat lady turned around. That's B.C.'s name for her. Mrs. Powers sits in the pew in front of us and wears a different hat—a big hat—every Sunday. Today's pink straw hat had tiny rosebuds all around the white band. On anybody else it would have looked silly, but not on Mrs. Powers. If she'd been a horse, she'd have been a cross between a Pinto and a Lippizaner, colorful and cool.

"Morning, Scoop," she said. "It's lovely to see your grandfather enjoying music in God's house. I can see your grandmother's work on him paid off."

"My grandmother's work?" I asked. I'd heard stories about Reba Mae Coop, but this sounded like one I hadn't heard.

Mrs. Powers whispered at me over her shoulder. Her white-gloved hand shielded her bright, pink mouth, as if she feared the pastor might try to read her lips. "Reba played the cello. And she sang like an angel! She used to drag your grandfather to symphonies. I guess it rubbed off on him."

Just when I thought I had Grandad Coop pretty much figured out, I discover he's a nut for classical music. The organ music stopped, but it must have kept going in Grandad's head. His hands kept conducting an invisible orchestra. I wondered if he heard Reba.

The rest of the service went pretty much without incident. B.C. got in trouble kicking the pews, but Mr. Zucker handled it. Grandad sang louder than he should have, but he stayed put. The sermon was on Proverbs 3:5–6, "Trust in the LORD with all your heart and lean not on your own understanding; in all your ways acknowledge Him, and He will make your paths straight." I copied it on my church bulletin in case Dotty wanted to take it to work and memorize it.

I hoped Carla was listening to the part about understanding. She didn't seem to understand how important our show was to the future of Horsefeathers. Otherwise she would have been helping us get her horse ready.

As soon as church was over, I tore out after Carla. "Carla!" I called, chasing her. She didn't turn around until we were outside on the church steps. "Hey, where've you been? I've been working Ham for you, but you need to run through the show routine."

"I've got to go," she mumbled.

"What's the matter with you anyway?" I asked. "Don't you care about Horsefeathers? Or Ham?"

"Back off, Scoop!" she said, her eyes narrowed to slits. For a minute, she looked like a different person, like the Carla I'd met the first day she moved to West Salem. I hadn't liked that Carla. She turned to go.

"Wait up!" I hollered. I planted myself in front of her. "Look, Carla," I said, trying to keep the anger out of my voice. "I'm sorry about whatever troubles you're having at home. If it's about sharing your parents with a new baby, I understand—"

"Mind your own business!" she said. "I was crazy to think I wanted a brother or sister."

So Dotty had been right. Carla had already seen the light and figured out what a pain brothers could be.

B.C. was yelling for me from somewhere inside the church. "Scoop! Scoop!" he screamed, his voice slicing through the sea of quiet conversations buzzing on the church lawn.

Carla gave a short laugh, the kind that comes out your nose, without taking in your eyes and mouth, a mean laugh. "Why on earth would I want a brother like B.C.?" she shouted. Then she ran down the steps and crossed the street.

I stared dumbly after Carla, shocked at how changed she was. I was thinking so hard, I didn't even notice when Stephen and Ursula came up behind me until Stephen cleared his throat loudly.

I wheeled around and saw the two of them holding hands. They wore matching gray suits, although hers had a short skirt.

"Buckingham trouble?" Ursula asked.

Stephen gave me a look filled with false pity. "Looks like poor Sarah's not just losing a horse; she's losing the rider as well."

13

We had to hang around at church while Dotty hand-delivered every little kid from the nursery. They all clung to her like they didn't want to go back to their real folks.

"Mrs. Barry," Dotty said, carrying a boy in a football jersey and long, wavy hair his mom probably couldn't bring herself to cut. "Ronnie was a doll, a real big boy." She handed over the 2-year-old who probably hadn't been all that good. He squirmed and kicked to get away from his mom.

Dotty called every parent Mr. or Mrs., and they all called her Dotty, as if she still had her Hy-Klas nametag pinned to her polka-dot dress. I didn't think that was right.

We came home to the smell of onions and burned beef. Dotty had put potatoes and onions and carrots in a roaster with a slab of chuck roast. By the time we got to eat it, everything in the roaster had melded together in a glob that stuck to the bottom of the pan.

As soon as I could get away from Dotty's Sunday dinner, I walked to Horsefeathers.

Orphan met me as I strolled up the lane. She stuck her head over the fence and whinnied. A light breeze blew white fluff from dandelions gone to seed, leaving stems half bald and half gray, like Grandad.

"I'm sorry about this horse show business," I told Orphan, scratching her chin and rubbing my face next to her soft cheek. "I know I promised you I'd never make you go through that horse show nonsense again. But I can't help this. It's our only chance to convince Mrs. Buckingham that Horsefeathers is the best place for her show horse. Having this stable show is speaking her language."

I stared directly into Orphan's big, brown eyes and knew she understood. She batted her thick, black eyelashes.

"Let's ride!" I whispered.

Orphan stood perfectly still while I swung myself up on her back. This was our freedom ride. With nothing but a halter on, Orphan could pick our route, our pace, our destination.

She started off prancing to get out of the paddock. I leaned over and unlatched the gate to the back pasture. We galloped through grass worn low with grazing. Orphan wound through the thickets, across the creek, and to the end of Grandad's properties. I slid off and undid the wire loop on the back post, pulling the wire fence away from the corner. Orphan walked through and waited for me while I put the fence back and replaced the loop. I swung up and we were off again.

With my eyes closed, I leaned forward on her broad neck. The wind blew her mane in my face as I breathed in sugar clover and grass. Somewhere in the distance, a train whistled long and hollow.

Orphan hit a dirt path and cantered faster. A blur of green raced by as if I were peeking out of the train window. I couldn't imagine where the cool air that brushed the hair on my arms came from. Orphan veered right and cantered up a steep hill. I felt as if these hills were God's house too—just like church. And I thought that if God decided to live in just one place, He might choose this spot, Orphan's and my secret place.

Without warning, Orphan stopped so suddenly I had to squeeze my thighs into her sides to stay on. Her ears rotated, then flicked back and forth, like antennae. I followed her gaze to a spot in the tall, dry grass where the long stalks had been pressed down. It looked like a giant field nest. As I stared at the swirl of golden weeds, a form took shape in the center of the nest. A fawn lay curled up beside her mother.

I felt a jarring deep in my soul, an awe of what God had let us encounter. I'd felt it before—at the sight of a rainbow, or the unexpected honking of geese flying over. It was as if

God had brought us here to let us in on one of His surprises.

The deer craned her neck around and stared with big, round eyes at Orphan and me—exactly as if God had made her for us, for this moment. Then Mama and her baby stood up slowly on long legs and walked—not ran—away.

"They're awesome, aren't they?" The voice startled me as much as the deer had, as much as if the fawn itself had spoken.

Travis Zucker got up from the tall grass under a nearby cottonwood tree. He carried a walking stick and had a backpack on his back.

I had felt like Orphan and I were the only ones around for miles. This was *our* secret spot. "But how ... " I stammered. "How ... did you find—?"

Travis smiled at me. "I've been coming here for years, Scoop. It's the perfect place to think or to quit thinking. I escape to this spot when I want to be alone." He flashed that smile that always melted Maggie 37. "But today ... I'm glad you were here. It was a good moment to share with someone."

Travis turned, and leaning on his walking stick, hiked over the hill and out of sight.

Orphan stood her ground. I leaned back, using her soft rump as a pillow and let the sun beat down on my face. Black shapes moved behind my eyelids. I might have dreamt Travis there. I could have imagined the doe and her fawn. It had all been too wonderful, too peaceful and perfect.

Then as suddenly as the appearance of the deer, as suddenly as the sound of Travis' voice, Carla flashed through my mind. I could see her face, her pursed lips. I could hear her say she'd never want a brother like B.C. Then I pictured Carla's mother, covered in mud. And my whole mood was ruined.

Orphan and I walked back to Horsefeathers. I kept my eyes opened for Travis, but he was gone, as if he'd never even been there.

~~~~~~~~~~~~~~~~~~~~~~~~~~~~~~

"There she is, Stephen!"

It was Ursula. She and Stephen were on horseback, sitting up straight in their English saddles just outside Horsefeathers' barn.

"Horsefeathers," I muttered.

Stephen Dalton, in tan jodhpurs and a white shirt, dug his spurs into his horse to trot toward me. Champion, Stephen's sorrel American Saddle Horse gelding, 17 hands high, flaxen mane and tail, had won titles in the three-gaited classes throughout the state.

Stephen lifted one rein in a weak waving gesture at me. "We were beginning to think Horsefeathers had turned into a ghost town. Or should I say, *ghost barn?*"

Ursula, laughing at Stephen's stupid joke, trotted up beside him, posting mechanically. She rode a coal black American Saddle Horse that had to be five-gaited. Next to her horse's sleek black coat, Orphan's sunburned coat looked reddish. Not that I cared. Her horse had to be cooped up in a stall all day out of the sun's rays to keep him so black. I'd never do that to Orphan.

"She's riding bareback, Stephen," Ursula said, as if I weren't there in person. "Isn't that cute?"

"Sarah Coop doesn't believe in saddles, do you, Sarah?"

"Are you lost?" I asked as pleasantly as I could muster.

"What?" Ursula looked confused. Her clothes were identical to Stephen's, right down to the tall, leather boots.

"We're not lost, thank you," Stephen said. "We thought you'd be practicing for *the big show* on Tuesday. We wanted to watch."

"Sorry," I said, hopping off Orphan. "No practice on Sundays. And besides, Horsefeathers' practices are not open to the public." I was starting to sound like Maggie 37.

"Ahh." Stephen tried to look disappointed, but it made him look like a bug-eyed frog. "Well, I guess we'll just have to wait for the real, live, Horsefeathers Horse Show, Ursula."

Horsefeathers, I thought, as they rode off, prancing side by side, bobbing up and down like twin pogo sticks. Now on top of everything else, I had to worry about those two coming to the show.

The rest of the day, I hung out with Orphan, hoping Maggie or Jen—or maybe Travis—would drop by Horsefeathers. I kept coming back to Carla and what she'd said in church. Maybe I should have barged into Buckingham Palace and demanded an explanation. Maybe if she'd talk about being a sister, she'd get back some of her old good feelings about it. I could tell her that *sometimes* having a brother wasn't so bad, that B.C. did help me through that awful time without our folks, that sometimes I couldn't imagine life without my brother.

But I didn't go. I didn't even call. I've never been too good with explanations—getting them or giving them. Some things are just too hard to understand. Maybe that's why Dotty's verse says that nobody does.

14

Monday is house chore day. So even though my whole life depended on the horses being ready for Tuesday's show, Dotty made me clean and do laundry.

B.C. did the sinks and bathtub before Dotty left for work. But the minute her old, blue Chevy rattled out of the driveway, he made a beeline for the door.

"B.C.! Don't you dare leave until you fold the towels!" I yelled.

"You're not the boss of me!" he shouted from the back step.

I heard his footsteps as he scrambled to the roof. I started after him but stopped before I got outside. It just wasn't worth the effort. Brothers!

From Grandad's room came wheezing snores. He didn't run on the same clock as the rest of the world. I'd heard him pacing downstairs in the middle of the night. After breakfast, he'd gone back to bed.

Standing in the kitchen, listening to Grandad's snores and B.C.'s scuffling on the roof made me feel empty inside. Empty and alone.

Dear God, I prayed, hearing my prayer voice in my mind and wishing I could talk to God as natural as Dotty. *The more I do, the more it seems I've got to do. Tomorrow is that show Maggie got us into, and Carla and Ham haven't practiced at all. But we've just got to keep Ham at Horsefeathers. Okay?*

By the time I finished house chores, it was mid-morning. I ran most of the way to Horsefeathers. Panic as small as a pin prick in my chest grew into an open wound. Before the barn came into view, I knew something was wrong.

I stepped into the lane expecting to hear Orphan's nicker, or at least her hoofbeat as she trotted to meet me. But she didn't come. Instead, I heard voices and choppy, scraping sounds coming from the paddock.

Maggie and Jen were leaning over the top rail, staring into the paddock behind the barn. Orphan still hadn't come.

"Orphan!" I hollered.

Maggie jumped from the fence and came running toward me, waving her green cowboy hat in the air. "Scoop! We thought you'd never get here!"

My feet stopped, and my heart thumped hard against the pain in my chest. "Is it Orphan?"

"What?" Maggie said, jogging up to me. "No, Scoop. Nothing's wrong with Orphan. She's fine."

"Are you sure, Maggie? Tell me the truth! Where is she? Where's Orphan?" My fingernails had dug little half-moons into the palms of my hands. I opened my fists.

"Orphan's in the paddock. She's watching too. She's fine, Scoop. Honest!"

A wave of relief rushed through me, covering my panic. Orphan was all right. "So what is it, Maggie? Why so dramatic?"

"It's Carla—and Ham."

"Carla's here?" I asked. "It's about time. Did you explain her part in the show tomorrow?"

"Not exactly," Maggie said, locking arms and pulling me toward the paddock arena. "I tried, Scoop. Only something's not right."

Maggie and I joined Jen on the fence. Jen wore a broad-brimmed, straw hat to keep the sun off her pale, white skin.

"I was just about to go get you, Scoop," Jen said, frowning over at me. She nodded to the arena, where Ham was prancing along the rail.

Carla Buckingham looked dressed for the show in her tall boots, khaki jodhpurs, and bowler. Her scowl cut so deep into her face that she looked older. She didn't even glance our way as they trotted by.

White lather covered Ham from his neck to his flanks and foamed at his tail. His wide eyes darted my way, and I sensed his panic and frustration. Tension made his shoulder muscles twitch.

"What does she think she's doing to that horse?" I cried. "Doesn't she have an ounce of horse sense? She's got him so confused, he's losing it!"

Jen put her hand on my arm. "Maggie and I tried to get her to let up or slow down or wait for you, but she acts like we're not here. And Scoop, she's using that crop again."

I looked harder at her hands and saw it, a short, black leather whip, the loop slipped around her wrist. Two seconds watching made me break out in a lather. Carla jerked the reins hard left, but tilted her body right, sending Ham mixed signals.

"Get ... up ... here!" Carla spat out each word to her frustrated horse.

"Carla!" I shouted. "Ham doesn't need the crop. He's wound too tight. Why don't you—"

"She won't listen," Maggie said.

Carla shifted her weight in the saddle just as Ham broke into a canter. He switched leads, thrusting out the outside leg first. That made Carla madder and she flicked the crop on Ham's inside shoulder. I knew it didn't physically hurt Ham, but I couldn't stand seeing him punished for something that wasn't his fault.

"Poor Ham!" Maggie exclaimed. "Do something, Scoop!"

I felt Ham's frustration, wanting to please Carla but not able to. Why couldn't she understand what she was doing to him? Orphan stood off in the corner of the paddock, looking as agonized as I felt.

Carla stared straight ahead as she and Ham galloped past, flipping clods of dirt at us. The acrid smell of horse fear covered me like lingering smog as they lumbered by us. Carla's heels dug into Ham's sides, but she jerked on the reins.

I couldn't take it anymore. I had to stop them. Ham was coming around again at a canter. I put my foot on the second rung of the fence to swing my leg over, but I bumped Jen's sun hat. It sailed off her head and into the paddock just as Ham got to us. He shied, jerking away from the floating hat. Ham's front legs went straight. He came to a dead stop a foot from me as I pushed off the fence and landed in the dirt.

Carla glared at Jen, then at me.

"Maybe Ham needs a rest," I said, trying to sound calm. Ham had never been this worked up—not since I'd known him. He snorted and tossed his head, flinging beads of sweat.

Carla ignored me. She pulled her horse into the center of the paddock ring and made him stretch out, setting his forelegs farther and farther from the hind legs.

I bit my bottom lip and walked up to them. First I'd see that Ham settled down. Then I'd have to try to talk to Carla. She had to get herself together—and fast.

Carla carefully dismounted and threw the reins to me. "Cool him down," she said, not even glancing at me.

The way she said it made me feel like a stable boy about to be fired. The humiliation burned in my throat.

Maggie ran over. "Did I just see what I thought I saw? What's with Little Miss Carla Buckingham, III?"

I shrugged. I wanted to feel angry, like Maggie, but the hurt flared up too strong, and embarrassment burned too deep. I'd actually thought of myself as Carla's friend—not just as her employee.

Jen joined us, brushing off her battered straw hat. "I do not understand that girl," she declared.

"I understand her all right," I said. "She's mad at her parents and she's jealous of this baby, so she's taking it out on Ham." And on me, I thought.

"Maybe her parents really are getting a divorce like I said all along," Maggie said.

Jen's analytical side kicked in. "You know, maybe she blames the baby, like she thought a baby would bring her parents together. But in reality the baby has driven them farther apart—the last straw, forcing them to go through with the divorce. I've read about that happening."

"Are you making excuses for her?" Maggie accused.

"No," Jen said. "I'm just attempting to gain some understanding." She turned to me. "What do you think, Scoop?"

I shrugged and led Ham toward the barn. I understood Carla Buckingham well enough to wish I'd never met her.

Maggie and Jen rehearsed their parts for the Horsefeathers Show while I cooled Ham down, walking him over the yards. I heard bits and pieces of Maggie's script as Jen rode Cheyenne in the arena. But the whole idea of a Horsefeathers Horse Show seemed ridiculous.

I spent a long time brushing Ham and trying to talk him down, but I couldn't get him calm. He pressed against the stall, sandwiching himself in. His eyes still looked glassy, and he jerked his head toward every little sound. Finally I gave up and turned him out to the private pasture.

"Ham is so wound up," I told Jen when she led Cheyenne to the cross-ties for brushing. "If he acts like this tomorrow night, Mrs. Buckingham will pull him from Horsefeathers for sure. It's Carla's fault. She's upset, so he's upset. What does she expect?"

"And all because of a brother or sister who hasn't even been born yet," Jen said. Cheyenne and Orphan nickered at each other through the barn wall. I hadn't even had time to brush Orphan yet, much less ride her.

Jen handed me a hoof pick and I started on Cheyenne's left front hoof, cleaning out the frog.

"Anyway," Jen said, brushing Cheyenne's withers until the Paint groaned with pleasure, "you can take it from me. This sibling rivalry thing can be intense—even when your parents don't get divorced on you. I already had Travis when Mom got pregnant with Tommy, but I was still miserable when they told me. I remember thinking my parents couldn't possibly have enough love to split three ways. By the time the twins were born though, I'd figured out that Mama and Papa Zucker had plenty of love to go around. Was it like that with B.C.?"

"I don't remember much pre-B.C.," I said, coming over to her side to finish off Cheyenne's hooves. "But my brother has always gotten the lion's share of attention."

Cheyenne caught us both with her tail, taking turns switching us. "Sibling rivalry or not," I said, dodging that quick sorrel-and-white tail, "Carla should know enough not to take it out on her horse."

"Carla will get used to the idea again," Jen said. "Give her time."

"We don't have time," I said. "Tomorrow's our only chance to keep Ham." I closed my eyes and stood up straight, stretching my aching back. The heat of the barn pressed at my skin. Could it possibly have been less than a month ago that I started Horsefeathers? The agony I'd felt when I thought I was losing everything returned in all its force.

Dear God, I prayed. *There is no one who understands. Don't let me lose everything all over again.*

113

Carla isn't coming! I told you she wouldn't make it!" Maggie 37 Orange paced the barn walkway, her pointed-toe, orange cowboy boots squeaking with every step, like mice on parade. The fringe on her silky, orange pants and shirt swished from side to side as she wheeled and paced again.

I felt like pacing too. Only I couldn't afford the luxury. Orphan had gotten herself into something black and sticky and I'd been rubbing at it for 15 minutes to get it out.

"Look, Maggie," I said, when I heard her squeaks behind me. "This whole Horsefeathers Show was your idea. People are coming whether we're ready for them or not. Besides, you're the pro around here. You're the big actress."

"I know," said Maggie 37 with a brave sigh. "The show must go on!"

She pushed the stall door wide open, and a slight breeze squeezed in, bringing with it the scent of lavender. The evening already sounded like a cricket symphony although the sun had barely started to set.

"Twenty minutes to showtime," Jen hollered, emerging from Cheyenne's stall. "Cheyenne is all saddled and ready to run!"

I glared at her from where I still crouched over Orphan's white stocking, rubbing the last of the black stuff out. "Ready to run, Jen? How about ready to perform calmly on command? Ready to prove that I'm the horse gentler we claim I am?"

"That's what I said." Jen looked really pretty in a pale blue shirt Mrs. Zucker made special. Ribbons out of the same material held up her long, blond hair.

I wore what I always wore—jeans and a shirt. I'm not sure where Dotty picked up my gray shirt that looked like a Polo shirt, minus the pony. Dotty doesn't sew. And even if she did, she wouldn't have time.

"There," I told Orphan, setting down her white forefoot. "That will just have to do."

"Still no word from Carla?" Jen asked, peeking out of Orphan's stall at the arena.

"Word?" I asked, trying to remember which of the million things I had to do next. "I had word from Carla. Two words, to be exact. When I phoned her this morning, she couldn't come to the phone just now, but thanks for calling. This afternoon, she answered the phone. Her two words were: 'I'll come.'"

That had been the whole conversation. I had hoped she meant that she'd come to the barn right then and help us get ready. Now I'd settle for her coming in time for the show.

"What's Stephen doing here?" Jen asked, still staring out of the stall toward the arena.

Maggie ran over for a look. "And there! See, Jen? That's the Hurl-Something girl I told you about. Maggie slipped into her fake Southern accent. "Ooooh, they're holding hands! I think I'm going to hurl, myself!" She put one hand over her mouth and tore out of the stall as if she had to puke.

Smack! She nearly ran over Travis Zucker. Maggie 37 Orange's face flushed.

"Maggie?" Travis said, chuckling. "You're not having a case of stage fright, are you?"

Maggie's eyes grew moon-sized as she said evenly, Southern accent intact, "I am going to die."

Ray strolled up to Travis and nodded hellos to us. "No sign of Carla yet?" he asked.

I shrugged. "She said she'd be here."

"Ya'll know what?" Maggie said, recovered now. "I sure could use some help with my big white horse." She batted her long eyelashes. "Travis, Sugar, could you please give li'l ol' me a hand?"

I couldn't bring myself to look at Travis for some reason. My heart beat faster. I told myself it was because *I* had the case of stage fright.

Travis trailed off with Maggie, and I went to

work lining up last-minute tack for the show.

"Did you know Carla's mother is out there?" Ray asked.

For a minute I felt like hurling too. "Mrs. Buckingham? And Carla's not with her? I don't know what we'll do if Carla doesn't show up, Ray. What's with her?"

Ray shrugged.

A bang, clank, thud sounded on the roof above us. I heard Ham squeal and shuffle in his stall. The last thing that horse needed was to get spooked.

"What was that?" Ray asked.

"It's coming from the roof, Ray. You want to make an educated guess?"

"B.C.?" he asked.

I handed Ray Orphan's lead. "B.C.!" I growled.

I tore around to the willow tree and shimmied up to the roof, where B.C. sat with his boom box. "Benjamin Bottle Cap Coop, don't you dare!" I shouted.

He grinned up at me with the face of an angel. His skin is soft and pale and his eyes always look watery. He's small, even for a fourth grader. "I brought you this," he said, handing me the boom box.

He passed me a box about the size of an English saddle. I lifted the lid and saw a solid metal rectangle made of bottle caps. Wires ran from the bottle-cap contraption to the radio.

B.C. unwrapped a microphone on a long, black cord. "It's for the show, Scoop. It's a great speaker! I tried it out myself at home. You should have seen Grandad!"

I stared stupidly at the bottle caps, then at my brother. I'd never figure out the kid or his manic depression. "Horsefeathers! Thanks, B.C."

He looked away, then jumped to the willow tree and climbed down.

I clutched B.C.'s speakers and leaned over the roof. "Is Dotty here?"

"Nope. Mr. Ford called her to the store for inventory. I gotta go baby-sit Grandad."

I yelled thanks to B.C. again, then struggled down the tree and back to the barn. Maggie and Travis were waiting.

"Seven minutes, Scoop!" Maggie said, breathless.

I showed them B.C.'s invention.

"That boy is an absolute genius!" Maggie declared in her Southern accent.

"He's Tommy's age, right?" Travis asked. "And he rigged this up by himself?"

I focused on Travis' perfectly straight nose and nodded.

"Not bad," he said.

I wished Carla had been there to hear them say good stuff about my brother. I wanted their words to drown out hers: *Why on earth would I want a brother like B.C.?*

Travis and Ray got the sound system ready so

Maggie could broadcast from the barn entrance to the paddock.

I double-checked Orphan, Cheyenne, Moby, and Ham. The horses were set to go, but still no Carla.

"Three minutes to showtime," Travis said. He brushed my arm as he reached over me to scratch Orphan's ears.

I felt a little shiver, and tiny goosebumps broke out over both arms. I hoped Travis couldn't see them. And I hoped Maggie's crush wasn't contagious.

"Scoop," Travis said, turning to face me, his deep blue eyes shooting through to my stomach and his lips curving up to show the whitest teeth I'd ever seen. "Good luck. You're doing a great job with Horsefeathers. Everybody will see that tonight."

I wished I could have been Maggie and thought of just the right thing to say. *Travis, that means so much coming from you.* Or, *Travis I can't tell you how much your friendship means to me.* Or, *Do you have any idea the kind of goosebumps you give me?*

I swallowed and nodded to his back as he walked out to the paddock.

"Scoop!" Maggie's voice jarred me back. "The Queen Mother of England is here!" Maggie's new name for Carla's mother.

"I know, Maggie," I said, slipping the bitless hackamore over Orphan's velvety nose.

"Yes," Maggie said, "but did you also know that the Queen is standing between that horrible Ursula and Stephen?"

"Great," I muttered. "I'm sure those two will help point out how wonderful we are."

"Time to start," Jen called. She walked up and stroked Orphan's blaze. "We're a minute late already, Scoop. What do you want to do?"

I didn't know what to do. I tried to pray on the spot, like Dotty does, but I didn't even know what to pray. Carla and I were supposed to come first in the program. I should have known I couldn't count on her.

Maggie's acting lessons must have kicked in. A new air of confidence swept over her. "The show must go on!" she proclaimed. "Scoop, you and Orphan get out there and show them what Horsefeathers Stable is all about! Just follow my lead as I announce. Jen, when Carla gets here, send her out."

Even Jen looked relieved to have Maggie take over. "When we're not riding," Maggie said, "we'll walk around and greet the spectators. Don't forget my mom, Mr. Chesley, and Brats Squared." Maggie's new name for her two stepbrothers.

"But Carla and I are supposed to ride together. Won't it be funny—" I started.

"Just go! I'll change the script as we go along. It will be fine," Maggie promised. "Go! Go! Go! On with the show!"

16

I hugged Orphan tight, burrowing my face in her soft, warm neck. I could have stayed like that forever, smelling my horse and feeling her heat, shutting out everything else. But Maggie's voice was already blaring over the speakers, welcoming everybody to Horsefeathers' Stable, Home of the Backyard Horses.

I prayed a quick one, hopped on Orphan, and headed out to the paddock arena. Polite clapping started from my right as I took the rail and trotted around the ring. I glanced toward the applause and saw Ray, Travis, and Tommy Zucker.

I caught a glimpse of Maggie's mother in her long, colorful sundress. She looked beautiful and exotic with her hair pulled back, showing her dark skin and angular face. Farther down, the Chesley boys were throwing mud clods at each other, while their father tried to make them stop.

I tried to hone in on what Maggie was saying. She had a perfect announcer's voice, clear and smooth. B.C.'s invention worked great.

The sky was filled with purplish pink swirls,

like celestial cotton candy. I tried not to think about Mrs. Buckingham or Stephen and Ursula as I rode by them. But Ursula's perfume greeted me with every lap. Once I glanced over, but they didn't seem to be watching. Ursula was saying something to Mrs. Buckingham, who cocked her head to listen.

Maggie's voice came across so light and fun, it almost sounded like singing. "Sarah Coop, better known as Scoop, is the manager of Horse-feathers Stable. We're lucky to have our very own horse whisperer on duty here at all times. Scoop believes in *gentling* horses, rather than *breaking* them. Horses here perform well because they *want* to perform well—not because they're afraid of us. That's just one of the things that sets Horsefeathers apart from all other stables in the region. This is where a horse is free to be a horse."

With everybody looking at me, I wished I'd worn something better than blue jeans. "Come on, Orphan," I whispered, urging her into a gentle trot.

Maggie kept up a steady stream of monologue. She broke from time to time to tell Orphan and me to walk, trot, canter, or change directions. When I spaced out, Orphan took over and responded to Maggie's command, trotting or turning with no help from me.

"You'll notice that Scoop is riding bareback," Maggie explained. "Yet she sticks to her horse better than most riders do with the aid of saddles and stirrups. But bareback riding is restricted to Orphan and Scoop at Horsefeathers Stable. The rest of us here take advantage of the protective equipment and saddles at all times. We recommend you do the same. Will you canter Orphan for us, Scoop?"

Orphan heard Maggie or sensed me and broke into a gentle canter that I couldn't help enjoying, even surrounded by all the interference. We were doing okay. Still, I knew none of it mattered if Carla didn't show up. Mrs. Buckingham couldn't care less about Orphan and me. What she wanted was to see Buckingham's British Pride.

Maggie went on to explain Jen's special homemade horse feed. She rattled on about the natural water resources and pastures at Horse-feathers. "As all horses do, given the chance," she said airily, "our horses love the great outdoors. So we let them have the freedom to come inside their stalls or go out and graze in pastures when-ever they want, 24 hours a day."

I was passing Mrs. Buckingham when Mag-gie said this, and I heard Stephen say something and chuckle. Ursula shook her head, like she dis-approved of letting horses graze outside. I knew that at Dalton Stables the horses are locked in their stalls all day every day, unless they're being officially exercised. It was just one of the reasons that I didn't want Ham to go live there.

We cantered again. Maggie was stalling. She'd picked up a Scottish accent, although I didn't know how many in the audience were still tuned in. Half the Zucker children had wandered off, even Tommy. Good ol' Ray and Travis hadn't budged, but I saw Ray yawn as I cantered by.

If Carla had been there, Orphan and Ham's part in the show would have ended a long time ago. Orphan and I couldn't keep doing the same things over and over. I tried to signal Maggie, but she ignored me and launched into a Scottish rendition of how a young lassie like me ended up with a stable of her very own.

That did it. Enough was enough.

I pulled Orphan up in front of Maggie and jumped off.

"Let's give a big round of applause for Scoop, the Horse Gentler!" Maggie shouted into the microphone.

People did clap. Somebody whistled through his teeth. Ray? Or maybe Travis?

Maggie put one hand over the microphone and whispered. "Still no sign of Princess Carla!"

"Shhh!" I whispered, hoping B.C.'s speakers weren't too good. "Jen will have to go on next."

I led Orphan into the barn and left her to help Jen get Cheyenne ready.

After a grand introduction, Cheyenne and Jen came out of the barn at a canter. The Zuckers brought down the house cheering for their sister and her horse. Maggie commanded Jen to walk, trot, canter, and reverse, all the while entertaining the crowd with the colorful history of the sorrel-and-white Tobiano Paint.

I could have hugged Cheyenne and Jen Zucker. They were wonderful. If Ham could do that well, we'd be home free. I stood by the proud Zuckers, all eight siblings and two parents of them. Although I love being around their family, it always makes me a little sad. Even with everything I had in front of me to worry about, I couldn't help wondering what it would be like to have a full set of family, with real parents.

"I'm impressed, Scoop," Travis said, leaning forward and talking to me across a sea of little Zuckers, including a couple in Mrs. Zucker's arms. "I knew you were good, but not *this* good."

I felt hot and cold at the same time as I forced myself to smile back at Travis.

"What a horse!" exclaimed Mr. Zucker, who was standing on the other side of me. He looked as proud of Cheyenne as if she'd been another Zucker daughter. "Tell me please, Mrs. Zucker," he asked his wife, who was at that moment trying to get one of the twins to stop pulling her twin brother's hair, "who was it who said, 'No greater piece of the kingdom can be glimpsed than in the movement of a horse!'?"

"I can't recollect, Mr. Zucker," she answered, separating the twins.

Jen rode by at a canter and waved to us.

"You're a miracle-worker, Scoop!" Mr. Zucker proclaimed.

I only wished Mrs. Buckingham had been standing near enough to hear. She didn't even appear to be watching.

The Zuckers cheered every time Jen came around the ring. Cheyenne shied only once, when Tommy Zucker let out a whoop as they passed. But it was a good showing.

Travis followed me to the barn and took Cheyenne from Jen.

"Thanks, Travis," Jen said, dismounting and patting her horse. "Wasn't she tremendous?"

"You both were," Travis said, which I thought was pretty nice for a brother. Maybe I'd try to be a little nicer to B.C.

"Would you just put her in her stall for me, Travis?" Jen begged. "Just unsaddle her. And brush her. And—"

"I got it, Jen," Travis said, leading the Paint away.

Jen and Maggie and I huddled to figure out the next move.

"I'll buy us time with Moby," Maggie said. "I did want to save her tricks for the end—a grand finale. But we'll roll with the punches. Jen, follow the script, but give me a sign if Carla still hasn't showed. I'll keep going. And you'll just have to think up something to say."

"But ... what—?" Jen asked. But Maggie was already untying Moby and mounting her silver-studded saddle.

Jen took over at the microphone. A metal squawk, then a long, high squeal made everybody cover their ears. The next sound was Jen's blowing into the mike and asking, "Testing? Testing, please?" Her voice came out much flatter than Maggie's, but at least her fans burst into applause.

Maggie exploded into the arena at top speed on her gallant, white charger. Even Ursula and Stephen took notice and stared as Moby and Maggie flew around the arena, Maggie waving her orange hat in the air. Moby kept galloping, and Maggie stood on her knees in the saddle. The fans went wild! As soon as Moby slowed to a gentle lope, Maggie stood in the saddle, holding onto the saddle horn with one hand and waving at her grateful audience with the other.

After pulling into the center of the arena, Maggie gave a signal to Jen.

Jen cleared her throat over the mike, which sounded like a herd of wild mustangs trampling her. Then she asked, "Um ... Moby, can you tell us how old you are?"

Moby counted out her age, which took quite a while—23 pawings with the right foreleg. The crowd counted out loud along with Jen.

Next Jen asked, "So Moby, is Horsefeathers the best stable in the world?"

Moby nodded yes several times, her head bobbing up and down.

"Moby, would you ever want to switch to another stable, like ... oh, say ... Dalton Stables?"

Moby shook her head no violently, and the crowd laughed—most of them anyway.

I'd made my way over to Maggie's elegant mother. Her light laughter sounded like a bell ringing. She clapped with three fingers of her right hand tapping the palm of her left, making no noise I could hear.

Mr. Chesley laughed heartily and cheered through the whole performance. He'd taught us science in seventh grade and was one of the teachers who didn't yell at you for not getting it. I liked Mr. Chesley. Maggie was lucky to get him as a stepfather. I hoped Maggie's mom would keep him.

At Jen's command over the loud speaker, Moby found a red object, one of Maggie's cowboy hats slung over a fence post. Next, Jen asked Moby for a green object. Maggie clasped her hands behind her head while her horse searched the audience for something green. Moby stuck her big, white nose over the fence and nuzzled one spectator after another until she came to Tommy Zucker. She grabbed Tommy's green army cap in her teeth, snatched it off his head, and shook it. Everybody laughed like crazy—everybody except Tommy Zucker.

In the next 15 minutes, Moby pivoted left and right, reared on command, and danced. She backed up, bowed, sidestepped, and whinnied on cue.

The outside barn lights came on automatically, and wide-winged, furry moths flew circles around poles, bumping into yellow bulbs. I glanced in every direction, hoping to see Carla, but she wasn't there. She wasn't coming. I knew it. The least Carla could have done was to let me know.

What I couldn't figure out was why Mrs. Buckingham showed up. I watched her whisper back and forth between Ursula and Stephen. Maybe *she* knew where her daughter was.

Maggie had obviously run out of tricks. And Jen was running out of dialogue. I caught Mrs. Buckingham glancing at her watch ... again. I had to do something, and I couldn't wait much longer.

17

I closed my eyes and listened to Jen's matter-of-fact commentary over the loud speakers.

"Stirrups were invented in China in the fourth century," Jen droned, "but Western Europe didn't start using stirrups until around 700 A.D. The eighth century Frankish cavalry was far superior to the Persian and Byzantine. Why, you ask? Because of the stirrup. Knights could now fight at a gallop.

"Some of you may wonder where the expression *feeling his oats* comes from. It was the humorist Haliburtin who first used the phrase in 1843 for a lively horse."

If only I knew for sure that Carla wasn't coming, I could end this stupid show right now. I had to talk to Carla's mother. There was nothing else I could do.

I prayed God would give me the words to say and the voice to say them. Then I started around the ring, making my way to Mrs. Buckingham while Jen kept talking in a monotone that would have put caffeine to sleep.

"Oddly enough," she was saying, "the word *manure* come from the French word *manoeuvre*, 'to do work by hand,' or 'to cultivate ... ' "

I only half listened to Jen while I inched toward Carla's mother. I tried to force an understanding, sympathetic smile. I'd act concerned, not angry. Too bad I wasn't an actress like Maggie.

I edged past Travis, who gave me the thumbs-up sign. Tommy Zucker stuck out his foot and tried to trip me.

Mrs. Buckingham sighed as I came up. Ursula whispered something to her, and I heard the words " ... what you get for living in a small town." They both grinned, but not nice grins.

"Hello, Mrs. Buckingham," I said, trying to keep my voice from shaking, trying to be a Belgian workhorse with blinders that shut out Stephen and Ursula and anything else that would keep me from my duty. I cleared my throat, but before I could get a word out, Mrs. Buckingham beat me to it.

"When do Carla and Buckingham's British Pride perform?" Mrs. Buckingham asked.

I opened my mouth, but nothing came out except, "Huh?"

"I don't know how much longer I can stay," she said. "I only came to see *my* horse. Are Carla and Buckingham's British Pride ever coming out?"

She was asking *me* about Carla? Mrs. Buckingham had no idea her daughter wasn't at

Horsefeathers. Had Carla told her she was coming? Carla must have lied to both of us.

"Earth to Sarah!" Stephen said, leaning his face so close to mine that I could smell his fishy breath. The metal from his retainer combined with a tuna smell. I jerked my head back.

No way did I want to get in the middle of whatever was going on with the Buckingham family. Carla would blame me if her mother found out she wasn't where she'd said she'd be.

"Um ... er ... Buckingham's British Pride? When? Well ... after Moby," I finally said.

She sighed again, and I slipped away as fast as I could, before she could ask me any more questions. Now what was I going to do? I'd promised Mrs. Buckingham she'd see her horse. I hadn't left myself much choice.

I crossed the paddock and pulled the microphone out of Jen's hands just as she was launching into Christopher Columbus' voyage to America with horses on the Nina, the Pinta, and the Santa Something.

"Ladies and gentlemen," I shouted. The mike screeched worse than it had for Jen, and the thinning crowd covered their ears. "Please wait a moment and we'll have the final act of our show for you." I was horrified at the way my voice sounded, like a little kid's, more like B.C.'s voice than mine. "Don't go away. We've saved the best for last."

Maggie and Moby rode over, and Maggie slid off Moby's rump. I motioned Jen to follow us into the barn, away from the mike.

"Thank goodness!" Maggie exclaimed. She'd lost her accents. "I was dying out there!"

"I cannot believe the way I ad-libbed!" Jen said. "At first I couldn't think of a thing to say. Then it all came to me. I could have gone on for hours."

Maggie rolled her eyes. "That's what I was afraid of. Thank heavens Carla made it before you *did* go on for hours!"

"So where is Carla?" Jen asked.

They looked around.

"Scoop?" Maggie said. "Carla *is* here, isn't she?"

I didn't answer.

Jen's face turned whiter than white. "Scoop, what are you going to do?"

"I'm going to ride Ham," I said quietly. I wasn't sure when I'd made the decision, but it was my only move.

Jen and Maggie stared at each other.

"Maggie, go out and say something nice about Ham," I said, grabbing Ham's bridle off the hook. "But don't call him Ham!"

I scurried into Ham's stall and slipped his bridle on. He was tense, but I felt pretty sure he'd calm down as soon as I did. *Lord*, I prayed, *please give me the peace of Christ so I can calm down this horse.*

Out in the arena, I heard Maggie announcing Buckingham's British Pride. In her best British accent, she bragged about the show horse bay who'd chosen Horsefeathers Stable.

I gathered the reins and put one foot in the stirrup. "Easy, Ham," I murmured. I felt him relax.

"What do you think you're doing?" The voice was iron sharp and cold as steel.

My foot slipped out of the stirrup, and Ham sidestepped into his feed trough.

"Carla!" I exclaimed. "Horsefeathers! Am I glad to see you!"

Dressed in full riding habit, Carla Buckingham looked terrific. "That's my horse! I haven't given you permission to show him. Get out of the way."

She brushed passed me and mounted Ham, who refused to stand still. "Open the stall," she commanded.

I did as I was told. I could sense Ham's anxiety double. His ears flicked up and back, and his eyes bugged wide as frog eyes. "Carla," I called after her, "try walking him a bit first, until he calms down."

She showed no sign of hearing me and rode out without a glance back.

Maggie must have been shocked to see Carla ride out instead of me, but you'd never have known it to hear her announce. She didn't miss a beat. "And last, but of course not least—we always save the best for last—Carla Buckingham on Buckingham's British Pride! Let's give them a hearty hand!"

The crowd had dwindled, but people clapped. Ray whistled.

Ham looked gorgeous, and I hoped that counted for something with Carla's mother. But the horse also looked nervous—not just high-strung, but agonized. Like rider, like horse, I thought. I wanted to shout at Carla to make her calm down. I wanted to hug Ham and tell him everything would be okay and I was sorry he had to be in this stupid show.

Jen and I stood off in the corner of the paddock. "Where did Carla come from? Why was she so late?" Jen whispered, as we watched Ham prance in a circle along the railing.

"Horsefeathers, Jen," I said. "Don't ask me."

"Ham doesn't look right, does he, Scoop?" Jen asked.

I shook my head no. Ham's eyes looked moist at the edges, and every muscle twitched.

Jen elbowed me. "Shouldn't you go stand with Carla's mother?"

I gave Jen my no-not-that-*anything*-but-that look. But she was right. I made my way over to Mrs. Buckingham and squeezed in between her and Ursula. "Ham—Buckingham's British

Pride—really looks great, doesn't he?" I asked, as he swept by us so close we could hear his heavy breathing. Already his chest was soaked with sweat.

"He's a fine animal," Mrs. Buckingham said. "We wanted Carla to have the best. I have to admit, his coat looks good. Did you oil him?"

"No Ma'am," I answered. "It's the molasses and grains Jen uses in the feed. It's all natural."

This was going so much better than I'd expected. Mrs. Buckingham was talking to *me* now. She liked the way Ham looked. *Thank You, Lord*, I prayed.

"Is your horse always this nervous?" Ursula asked sweetly. She leaned forward and talked across me to Mrs. Buckingham, as if I weren't there.

"I was just about to ask the same thing," Stephen said. "The bay looks hyper to me. He didn't seem to ride like that in the West Salem show. How is he getting along with the other horses at Horsefeathers, Sarah?"

As if he didn't know! As if he hadn't spied on us enough to know Ham wasn't fitting in.

I shrugged. I didn't have to answer to Stephen Dalton. It was none of his business.

Ham cantered by us so close to the rail we all stepped back. A dirt clod flew up and hit Stephen in the face. "Ow!" he cried, wiping his cheek with his sleeve.

I felt horse sweat or saliva hit my arm when Ham sneezed.

"He does seem nervous, doesn't he?" Mrs. Buckingham said. "This little exhibition shouldn't phase him. He's been in hundreds of horse shows."

Ursula leaned in again, flipping back her long hair with a toss of her head. "Do you *really* have time to care for these horses all by yourself, Sarah? And you're not even 15 yet? That is so cute! Isn't that cute, Stephen?"

She made me feel as if I were 5 years old playing horsey with B.C. As much as Maggie disliked Ursula, she'd have to admit the girl had class and sophistication. I felt like a mangy mustang to her Lippizaner.

"The horses are my responsibility," I said. "But Maggie 37 Brown and Jen Zucker ... and ... other people ... help me with Horsefeathers." I didn't know if I should include Carla or not. Not lately anyway.

"I tried to get Dad to hire Sarah at Dalton Stables, but he only accepts professionals," Stephen said.

Yeah, right. If Stephen has ever asked his dad to hire *me*, I'll be a nine-legged Appaloosa.

Still looking good, Carla and Ham trotted by us. I kept sneaking glances at Mrs. Buckingham, and she seemed to like what she was seeing. Carla walked Ham around a couple of more times, then cantered.

Ursula stepped down from the fence. "I'd better be going," she said. "I need my beauty sleep."

I bit my tongue so I wouldn't say what I was thinking. I hoped Stephen would leave with her.

Suddenly Ursula screamed. "Get it off!" She stomped the ground and swiped at her hair.

Stephen rushed to her rescue. "What? What is it?" he asked, staring at her.

She shook all over. "I don't know! Get it off, Stephen!"

Stephen examined her hair. "I think it's a spider's web—"

Ursula let out a piercing cry just as Ham cantered by.

Ham stopped cold, then reared, his forelegs waving high in the air. Carla flew off the saddle and crashed in the dirt with a great thud.

18

I ducked under the fence and ran to Carla. Her hat had slid around her neck, and her cheeks were red coals. Carla clutched her crop in one hand. When I reached for her, she yelled at me. "Leave me alone!" Then she hauled back and threw the whip at her horse.

It missed. But Ham was so startled he took off running full speed.

"The fence!" I screamed.

Ham ran straight at the arena fence and didn't slow a bit. Mrs. Zucker screamed and tugged her kids out of the way. Ham sailed over the fence with a foot to spare. He landed with a *th-thump* on the other side and galloped off through the pasture. Tommy Zucker yelled after the horse. The Zucker triplets were wailing.

I couldn't believe it. I stared down at Carla. "How could you do that? Ham is terrified! It wasn't his fault! Don't you even care what happens to him?"

Mrs. Buckingham ran up and knelt by her daughter. "Honey, are you all right? Don't move.

Can you tell if anything's broken?"

Carla pulled away from her mother as if she'd been burned by the touch. "Leave me alone," she whispered. Then louder, "Everybody just leave me alone!"

I watched Carla walk out of the arena, with Mrs. Buckingham jogging after her. She'd just ruined her own horse, and she didn't even care.

Ray and Travis ran in from one side of the arena, and Jen and Maggie from the other. "Is Carla all right?" Ray asked.

"I don't have time to worry about Carla now, Ray," I said. "Her horse is my responsibility. I have to go get him before he hurts himself."

"Did you see the way he took that fence?" Maggie exclaimed.

"Of course she saw," Jen said. "Scoop, what do you want us to do?"

I whistled for Orphan. "I'm riding after Ham," I said.

"It's pretty dark, Scoop," Travis said. "Will you be all right?"

"Orphan knows that pasture." Orphan trotted out of the barn and came over to me. I started to swing up, but before I knew what was coming, Travis had lifted me off the ground and onto Orphan.

"Go on then. We'll follow you on foot," Travis said.

Orphan only had a halter on, so I hoped she

was reading my mind. "Come on, Girl," I said, squeezing in with my thighs and leaning low on her neck. "Catch him!"

Ray opened the gate. Orphan let out a whinny and took off. I held onto her mane as she sailed out the gate and cantered through the dark field over black twisted shadows and under pale moonlight. I didn't see the stream until we were right up on it. Orphan jumped, landing with deer legs, and I barely bounced.

Faster and faster we galloped until I could see Ham way ahead of us. As we got closer, I knew something was wrong, way wrong. Ham wasn't moving. He'd run all the way to Dalton Stables, almost a mile. But now he stood still, trembling.

Then I saw why. His back leg was caught in wire, the wire fence outside Dalton Stables. Ham must have been running so fast he hadn't seen the fence until it was too late.

Orphan stopped several yards away. I slid off and told her to stay. I moved toward Ham, but he pulled back. I stopped. "It's okay, Boy." I stood still for minutes that seemed like hours and talked to him. When I turned back, Maggie, Jen, Ray, and Travis were halfway across the pasture coming toward us.

"Easy, Ham," I said, edging closer a step at a time. I had to move in tiny steps or Ham would struggle, tightening the tangle of wire around his pastern. "I'll get you out."

I tried to see if the leg looked deformed or cut. I didn't see blood. Ham was shaking all over. So was I. My heart prayed without words—just pure feeling and pleading for help.

I glanced back. Travis had Orphan by the halter. "Be careful, Scoop," he whispered. "You don't know what that horse might do."

I heard Maggie's voice behind me: "Thank goodness that electric fence wasn't turned on!"

I knew the Daltons turned it off at night to save money since they lock the horses inside. If the electricity had been turned on, Ham might have been killed.

I reached for Ham, talking to him the whole time. He jerked back. The wire went *boing*. I backed off. It took three more tries before Ham let me close enough to help. But the wire was easy to pull off.

"Travis, come get Ham's reins!" I called.

Travis looked like he was taking on a fire-breathing dragon, but he got close enough to pick up the reins. I checked Ham's legs. His muscles quivered, but the legs looked okay, except for a couple of scrapes that would heal even if he wouldn't let me treat them. When I set down his hoof, Ham flinched and pulled away.

I took the reins from Travis, and Maggie, Jen, and Ray walked with us back to Horsefeathers with Orphan leading the way. As soon as we came in sight of the barn, Ham reared up. I held on to his bridle and was pulled down into the grass. Travis ran up and grabbed the reins from me so I could get to my feet.

"Easy, Ham," I said. "We'll take good care of you." Finally the horse came with me, but he hadn't calmed down much by the time we got back to Horsefeathers.

I turned him out by himself in the south pasture and let Orphan out with Moby.

We piled on top of each other in the pickup and Travis drove us home. Nobody said much, but I knew we were all thinking the same thing. There was no way the Buckinghams were going to keep Ham at Horsefeathers—not after this.

It was all Carla's fault. Selfish little Carla Buckingham had taken out her jealousy and anger on her horse. I wouldn't blame Ham if he never forgave her.

~~~~~~~~~~~~~~~~~~~~~~~~~~~~~~

The next day I didn't hear from Carla or her mother. I didn't need to. I knew they'd be moving Ham to Dalton Stables at the end of the month—less than a week away—or sooner.

"That poor horse," Dotty said, downing a slice of buttered toast at breakfast.

Grandad shuffled out to the kitchen in his striped pajamas, the top on backwards. He was humming along to a tune nobody else could hear.

"Good morning, Jared!" Dotty said, already putting food on his plate. She bent down and gave him a quick shoulder hug.

"Horsefeathers," he muttered, scowling at his plate and shaking off her hug.

I peered into his eyes, and it looked like he might be home. He also just might be my last hope for helping Ham. My grandfather had trained hundreds of horses in his day. He *must* have run into at least one horse that had been spooked as bad as Ham. What if he knew a secret about getting a horse over a nervous fit? I had to find out.

"Grandad?" I said.

Without looking up, he reached across the table for the butter.

I tried again. "Grandad, last night Carla Buckingham's horse got scared—really scared—by Carla. Then he dumped her, ran off, jumped the fence, and got tangled up in Dalton's wire fence."

"Mmmm," he mumbled, putting enough butter on his toast to fry potatoes.

I couldn't tell if he meant, "Mmmm, very interesting, tell me more," or if he was just humming.

"What I'm wondering is if you know any cures for a horse that's lost trust. I have to work fast because he's going to Dalton Stables."

Grandad bit his toast. Butter stuck to his lip

like a creamy yellow mustache.

He didn't seem to hear me. I was just about to give up and decide Grandad wasn't home after all when he muttered something.

"You say something, Grandad?" I asked.

"Cookies," he mumbled.

I wasn't sure I heard him right. "Cookies? Did you say cookies?" I glanced to Dotty for help, but she was packing B.C.'s lunch and not paying us any mind.

Grandad stared at his toast as if a secret message were written in those butter peaks. "Chocolate chip cookies, Reba's secret recipe."

The chair squealed against the grayed linoleum as I scooted my chair back and got up. Grandad wasn't home. And I was on my own.

19

Buckingham's British Pride refused to come in for his feed. When I finished the rest of the barn chores, I took a bucket of Jen's best mash and headed for the back pasture. Ham didn't let me come within 50 feet of him. Finally, I left the bucket and went back to exercise the other horses.

Around noon, Maggie showed up in regular jeans and a T-shirt that said *Kennsington Summer Stock Theater*. "What are you going to do about Carla, Scoop?" she asked, whipping out a lump of sugar for Moby. "Will they at least leave their horse here until the end of the month?"

I brushed Cheyenne harder. "At this rate, they won't be able to catch their horse by the end of the month."

"Jen says she's read about horses that go sour and nobody can ever get them back," Maggie said. She made Moby bow for the second lump of sugar. "Wouldn't that be horrible, Scoop? And to have it happen here at Horsefeathers?"

Maggie hugged Moby's neck. Her tiny black

braids spread across Moby's white neck, like a spider on snow. I tried not to think about Ursula and her spider attack and everything that came after it.

"You know better than anyone," Maggie said, "that Ham has never been my favorite gelding. But I'd never do what Carla did to him last night."

"She didn't actually hit Ham with the crop," I said.

"Tell Ham that," Maggie said. "It just makes me so mad! I don't care if her parents *are* breaking up or if she's going to have a hundred little brothers. That doesn't give her the right to treat her horse—and us—like dirt!"

Cheyenne crooked her head around at me to tell me I'd spent enough time brushing the same spot.

"Sorry, Cheyenne," I said, moving around to her other side and stroking her forelock on the way. "Ham won't let me near him, Maggie. He's the one I'm going to try to figure out. Not Carla."

~~~~~~~~~~~~~~~~~~~~~~~~~~~~~

Maggie and I rode Moby and Orphan in the afternoon. It helped clear my head, but as soon as my feet touched ground again, I went back to worrying about Ham. I tried one last time to get him to come in, but he snorted and galloped away, pacing the far fence, with his tail held high.

I decided to stop by the Hy-Klas and say hi to Dotty on my way home. The little bell over the door clinked as I stepped inside. Mr. Ford actually had the air conditioner running—not a lot, but cooler than outdoors for a change.

I heard a frail, high-pitched voice hollering at Dotty. A thin, bent woman with bluish-gray hair was holding up Dotty's checkout line. "Paper! Not plastic!"

"I'm sorry, Ma'am," Dotty said in her cheery voice. "Let me change them groceries for you." She emptied the two plastic bags, item by item onto her counter. Then she whipped open a brown paper grocery bag and started placing them in one at a time.

"How much did you charge me for that?" The woman pointed a crooked finger at a small package of white napkins.

The lady behind her let out a huge, loud sigh. Her little boy squirmed in the front of the shopping cart and pulled a pack of gum from the temptation rack, Dotty's name for the strategically placed racks up by the checkout line, where customers are lured into buying out of boredom.

"Seventy-nine cents," Dotty said, pulling the package of napkins out of the brown bag, where she'd just repacked it.

"I knew it! You cheated me! It's 39 cents.

Thought I wouldn't notice, didn't you? An old lady like me?"

I felt my face grow hot. That woman didn't have a clue about Dotty. Dotty is the most honest person in the whole, wide world.

Dotty's smile looked warm and even like she felt sorry for the woman who'd just accused her of cheating. "Well, let's see here. This here bar code can mix up something awful."

Dotty looked up the price on a list behind the counter. "Hmmm," she said, as if she were as surprised and puzzled as the old lady. "Tween you and me, that there little bit of napkins had *oughta* cost 39 cents. But it ain't. It's 79 and—"

The woman pushed the package at Dotty. "You can keep it!" she said.

I couldn't watch anymore. As I sneaked back outside, I heard Dotty talking sweetly about the high cost of putting food on the table these days.

A film of sadness clung to me as I walked out into the blazing heat. I climbed up to the grocery store roof to think. The black shingles were way too hot to sit on, but I found a good spot on the back side of the roof. I'd done a lot of thinking up there in my time. So had B.C.

How could anybody say that stuff about Dotty? If they had an ounce of horse sense and understood her like I did, they'd be sorry. Again, Dotty's waterlogged verse popped into my head: *There is no one who understands.* No kidding.

I understood Dotty, but I was the only one who did.

And Carla? I understood her too. She was rich and she didn't want to share the little pieces she got of her parents with a baby brother or sister. I guess I understood her well enough—well enough to steer clear of her from now on.

I tried to pray, but even though I was closer to heaven up on the roof, I couldn't seem to get through. Finally I climbed down from the Hy-Klas roof and walked home.

~~~~~~~~~~~~~~~~~~~~~~~~~~~~~~~

"Horsefeathers, Girl! Take yer shoes off outside, Scoop!" Grandad barked at me the minute I stepped into the kitchen.

I was so shocked to see him acting normal, I obeyed.

"Grandad's *really* home," B.C. whispered. I wondered if either one of them realized they were dressed exactly alike—blue jeans and green plaid shirts. They even had twin milk mustaches. They were sitting at the kitchen table with a huge, beat-up scrapbook opened in front of them. The thing took up half the table.

Grandad got up and poured a glass of milk. He sat back down at the table and set the glass in front of the empty chair. B.C. nodded to me to drink it. I took a sip, even though I hate milk. It was warm and tasted like melted chalk.

I sat across from them and looked upside down at the brownish photographs stuck to musty black paper by green paper triangles at the corners. "What are you looking at?" I asked.

"Guess who this is," B.C. said, pointing to a picture of a skinny, shirtless kid in baggy pants. I got up and walked around the table to look over B.C.'s shoulder. The kid in the photograph had an ornery look, like he'd just pulled off some prank.

"It's Grandad!" B.C. said, unable to wait another second to show me he knew something I didn't.

I stared at the cute kid with wavy, bushy brown hair, then at my grandfather, his tufts of gray sticking out of his balding head. It didn't seem possible they were the same person.

Grandad flipped the book over a bunch of pages to a picture of a pretty girl who didn't look much older than me. She was holding a baby wrapped up in a blanket. Grandad touched the cheek of the girl in the photo. "Reba," he whispered. Then he added, "Benjy."

A lump formed in my chest and spread to my throat so I couldn't breathe without making a raspy noise. *Benjy*. That's what Grandad called my dad, Benjamin Coop. I was looking at a photograph of my grandmother holding my dad.

B.C. swung around to look at me. He had tears in his eyes.

I pulled up the stool on the other side of Grandad. "Show us more, Grandad," I asked.

He turned several pages. B.C. scooted in closer. Grandad stopped at the wedding picture of Benjamin and Emma Coop, my parents. I had the same picture on my dresser. Below that was a picture of my mom, still in her short, plain, white wedding dress, and a girl in a green satin bridesmaid dress.

"Is that Dotty?" I asked. The face looked the same, but she had tiny wire-rimmed glasses instead of the thick brown ones she wore now. She was short, but only a tiny bit overweight.

"Wow!" B.C. said. "She was pretty!"

Grandad sniffed and flipped back a page. He pointed to two girls who had to be my age or even younger. They were laughing, their arms locked at the elbows. They could have been my classmates. "Dotty and your mama," Grandad said.

I stared at them, wishing I could hear their laughter, almost hearing it.

Grandad started to turn the page, but I stopped him. I'd almost missed the picture tucked at the bottom of the page.

"Who's that?" I asked. "Who's with Dotty?" Dotty looked a little older than she did in the picture with my mom. Standing next to her, staring down at her like he thought she was Miss America, was a tall, very cute guy. He reminded me of a Tennessee Walking Horse, with long legs and long everything, kind of like Ray.

Grandad scratched his head. "Bo … Bo Somethin'. They was engaged to marry."

I didn't hear what he said next or what B.C. asked. Dotty engaged? In all the years she'd looked after B.C. and me since my parents died, I'd never once thought about her being married. She'd been engaged! What had happened to the boy in the picture? Horsefeathers, what had happened to the *girl* in the picture? Dotty had been engaged to marry. And not an hour earlier I had thought I was the only person on earth who really knew my aunt.

Maybe I didn't understand as much as I thought I did.

20

Grandad was still *home* when Dotty got back from the Hy-Klas. You'd have thought he was her long-lost best friend, the way she soaked up every coherent word he said. Twice I caught her wiping tears away when she thought we weren't looking.

We all stayed up later than usual. B.C. got into one of his talky moods and chattered non-stop. I wanted to ask Dotty about the boy in the scrapbook, but she wouldn't sit still long enough. Dotty never sits for too long at a time. Just when I'd get control of the scrapbook and turn to the page with her fiancé on it, she'd be off wiping the counter or making fresh decaf.

Finally I told Grandad goodnight and headed upstairs to bed. I was halfway up when I heard him say something. I turned back. "Did you say something, Grandad?"

"How're them horses, Scoop?" he asked, not taking his eyes off his hands.

"They're good, Grandad," I said, amazed at how he could come and go in his own body like that. "Orphan's the same—wonderful." I walked back to the living room and waited for him to make some crack about my orphaned horse, the only mixed breed he'd ever had in his stable. But he didn't.

That gave me enough of a hope to try asking him one more time about Ham. "Grandad," I said, squatting down in front of him to try to look into his eyes. B.C. had gone to bed, and Dotty was taking a bath, so I had Grandad all to myself. "Did you ever train a horse that got so frightened by his rider he wouldn't let anybody near him?"

Grandad was silent so long I thought maybe he'd gone away again. He rocked, making the only sound in the room. Then he nodded. "Yep. A couple."

"How did you get them back? How did you make them trust you again?"

"Chocolate chip cookies," he said, grinning.

My hope fizzed out. It was the same stupid answer he'd given that morning.

"Goodnight, Grandad," I said, getting to my feet.

"Reba's secret recipe." He said it as if he were watching his childhood bride make a batch of cookies right there. "She could never get Patty to help in the kitchen. That girl was a stubborn one."

I stopped. Patty? He must have been talking about Patricia, now Patricia Dalton, Stephen's mother. I'll bet it had been a long time since anybody had called her Patty. She and my dad were sister and brother, but they had some kind of falling out nobody ever told me about. Maybe they just didn't get along as grown-ups ... or as kids. Good ol' sibling rivalry strikes again.

Grandad stopped rocking. Outside an owl hooted. "Then Reba started making her *secret* chocolate chip recipe. 'Patty,' she'd say, 'now you stay out of this kitchen, you hear? I'm making my secret recipe. Don't you come in here!' And before Reba had all the fixin's set out, Patty would be sneaking into her kitchen. Reba acts like she's having such a fine time she don't see when Patty starts in helping."

Grandad chuckled, and I did too. I wondered at how sometimes he could forget his wife had been dead for 20 years, and other times he could remember something like this. What happened in his brain to make him think of chocolate chip cookies whenever I asked him about helping a troubled horse?

Grandad finally looked at me, narrowing his eyes as if studying a zit on my nose. "Horsefeathers, Scoop. You bake them cookies at the barn. That horse'll come around." Then he stood up so suddenly I fell backwards from my squat and landed on my hind end.

Grandad didn't seem to notice. He hummed

to himself as he hobbled to his room and shut the door.

~~~~~~~~~~~~~~~~~~~~~~~~~~~~~~~

The next morning I couldn't remember my dream. But when I woke up, three things had come together in my mind: music, Ham, and chocolate chip cookies.

While B.C., Dotty, and I ate our bowls of Tastee-O's, I tried to explain what Grandad had told me about the secret cookie recipe.

"If that don't beat all!" Dotty said between spoonfuls of Hy-Klas Choco Crisps. "Ain't Jared the smart one!"

"I think that if I can make Ham believe I'm having as much fun as Grandma Coop did baking cookies, maybe Ham will want to come closer and see what I'm doing—just like *Patty* did for Grandma Reba. Then maybe she'll start trusting me."

"I don't get it," B.C. said. "How can you bake cookies in the barn?"

"I'm not actually going to bake cookies, B.C.," I explained. "But it's the same idea. I've got a bunch of ideas how to lure Ham in. Music, for one. I just hope Ham can hear my radio in the back pasture." I checked the batteries of my tiny transistor radio, the only one I had. It had come inside a stuffed horse Dotty gave me for Christmas one year.

B.C. disappeared and returned with his

boom box. He handed it to me and went back to his cereal.

"What's this, B.C.?" I asked.

"He'll hear this," he said. "I rigged up the extra speakers myself. You could put a tape there or use the radio. My speakers work for both."

I'd never figure out B.C. There was no middle ground with my brother. *When he was good, he was very, very good. And when he was bad, he was horrid.* The doctor called it manic depression, but to me it was just B.C.

The last time I'd heard B.C.'s music blaring from that boom box, I'd wished he'd never been born.

"You're a genius! Thanks, B.C.," I said, scruffing his head. "I take it all back. I'm glad you were born."

He tried not to smile, but I saw his dimples.

~~~~~~~~~~~~~~~~~~~~~~~~~~~~

"What a great idea!" Maggie squealed. "I'll bring tapes. What about rap? Or show tunes! Ham won't be able to resist *Showboat* or *Oklahoma*. Maggie had just stopped by the barn on her way to piano lessons. She helped me set up the boom box and the stage, my cookie factory, in Ham's stall.

Orphan looked on while we scurried around setting out oats, plastic balls and rings, water, and a couple of projects for me to work on. She nuzzled the balls, but I kept her from eating all the oats. "You've had yours, Orphan. This is for

Ham." Still, I couldn't help giving her a handful.

"Good luck!" Maggie said. "Sorry I have to go, but Miss Tibbits will kill me if I'm late for piano again. I'll try to stop by later."

Maggie left, and Orphan wandered out in the pasture to graze with Moby. I opened Ham's stall door wide to the back pasture. I could see Ham ... and he could see me. I was as nervous as if this were a real, live performance. In a way it was. I prayed that it would work.

In front of the barn, a car door slammed. I knew from the footsteps, before he stuck his head in, that it was Travis.

"Scoop?" he called.

I hated the way my throat closed whenever I was around Travis. I cleared it. "In here!" I'd set up a saw horse and Grandad's old saddle, so I started in on it with saddle soap.

"Hey," he called.

I turned and saw that Travis was carrying a big, orange Tabby cat.

"Horsefeathers," I muttered, dropping the sponge and meeting Travis in the stallway. I took the cat from him, which he seemed to appreciate. He wiped his hands on his jeans, and I noticed that even his fingers looked tanned, perfectly golden brown.

"Jen and I were talking about your trouble with Ham," Travis said. "Jen read somewhere that horses who don't take to other horses will sometimes bond with a companion animal. The book suggested a goat or a peacock, but it said a cat might work. I thought it was worth a try. So, Madam Scoop, I'm pleased to present your official Horsefeathers mascot."

"I can keep it?" I asked. Already the cat purred her own brand of music. "I mean, we can keep her at Horsefeathers?"

"About time you had a barn cat," Travis said, stroking the cat in my arms. "We'll never miss her. We've got more cats than kids at the Zucker menagerie, if you can believe that."

The cat closed her eyes and moved into my touch wherever I petted her. "Thanks, Travis," I said. I fetched a handful of horse mash and set it out in a pan. The cat sniffed it, then took a piece and chewed, mouth open, just like B.C.

Travis looked around Ham's cluttered stall. "What's going on here?" he asked.

"Here?" I said. "I'm just baking chocolate chip cookies." I explained all about Reba and Patty and Grandad's theory of winning back Ham. As we talked, I almost forgot he was a guy and 16 and handsome.

"Wait here," Travis said. He ran out of the barn and I heard his truck door slam. For a minute, I was afraid he was going to leave. But when he came back, he had a handful of cassette tapes. "Most of these are Jen's," he said. "They're all classical, so maybe they'll help calm Ham."

I thanked him and popped Vivaldi's *Four Seasons* into B.C.'s tape player. The new Horse-feathers cat curled up on the hay in the corner of Ham's stall, as if she'd lived there all her life. I hoped this comfortable atmosphere was catching. I peeked out at Ham, but he stayed in the back of his pasture, not even looking our way. I turned up the music.

Travis hung around while I soaped the saddle. We talked about school and teachers, his brother Tommy and my brother B.C. He told me a joke about canaries. I'd heard it before, but I laughed anyway because it was still funny.

After Travis drove off, I prayed. I needed to be totally calm and peaceful. Ham would read my body language and pick up on things I didn't even see in myself. I turned up the music, and Orphan trotted over to see what I was up to. I stepped outside with her, where I was sure Ham could see us. Then I laughed and fussed over her, knowing that horses love laughter.

After that, Moby and then Cheyenne visited me while I cleaned Ham's stall. Every couple of minutes, I stepped out into the pasture with them and twirled and laughed. I tossed the ball to Moby and she bounced it back with her nose. And all the while, I acted as if I'd never had more fun in my whole life.

Ham inched closer. He knew something good was going on, but he wasn't about to investigate. Our new Horsefeathers mascot curled up on an outside post not far from Ham, as if the cat were in on the whole secret recipe.

At the end of the day, Ham still hadn't come into the stall, but he was definitely curious. His ears pricked more and more in my direction, and I caught him swinging his head to peer into his stall.

"You watch out for Ham now, Orphan," I told her as I left for the night. "And keep an eye on ... on ... Cat." We'd have to come up with a name for the cat, but I was too tired to think of one.

That night I went to bed early. I'd been dying to tell Grandad about baking cookies at the barn like he said, but he was already in bed when I got home. B.C. said he'd been there all day.

I turned out my light and lay in bed. Ever since the disaster at the Horsefeathers show, I'd concentrated on helping Ham, knowing that at the end of the week, the Buckinghams would cart him off to Dalton Stables. Now, in the stillness of my room, other thoughts and fears crowded in. What was going to happen to Horsefeathers when Ham left? What would happen when word got around that I'd failed with the Buckinghams' show horse? A surge of panic raced through me like an electrical shock.

I tried to pray, to toss everything up to God the way Dotty does. But the questions were lead weights on my chest, pushing me down, down, down until I finally fell asleep.

21

The next morning I started in again before the sun made it past the treetops. The sky shone a white-pink as I walked to Horsefeathers. It made me think of a watercolor B.C. had painted in third grade. His art teacher gave him a C– and told him that his sky was too white, that it didn't look real. I hoped B.C. *and* the art teacher were looking up now.

Ham kept his "safety space" all morning, hanging back about 10 yards from the stall, his rump toward me. Our new Horsefeathers mascot greeted me and ate the scraps I'd brought for her. Then she regained her post—the fence post closest to Ham.

I exercised Cheyenne and had a great ride on Orphan before putting them both out to graze in the east pasture with Moby. I didn't want Ham to have to pass through Moby, Cheyenne, and Orphan to get to the "chocolate chip cookies."

Rummaging through the tapes Travis left me, I found one with instrumental hymns. I popped in the cassette and sang along while I did chores.

By the time I got done cleaning stalls, Ham had taken several steps toward me.

I switched from singing to talking and kept up a steady stream of chatter that would have matched B.C.'s talky moods. "It won't be long now, Ham," I said, not looking directly at him, but keeping my voice loud so he could hear me. "Today I brought along a book. I'll read to you if you're real good. You want to come closer and smell the cookies? Well, I'm sorry. You can look, but this recipe is top secret, handed down to me by my grandad."

After a couple of hours, Ham turned to face me. The cat rubbed against the horse's hooves. I was afraid Ham might step on the cat, but he seemed to look out for her instead.

In the afternoon, Maggie and Jen came by. "Guess what I heard!" Maggie exclaimed before I could tell her to lower her voice. Ham took a few quick steps backwards and moved to the back of the paddock.

I needed a break anyway. My legs were stiff from sitting cross-legged in Ham's stall, reading *Man O' War* out loud. I stood up and shook a charley horse out of one leg, stretching my aching back. "Okay, Maggie," I said, "what did you hear?"

"The Buckinghams really are getting a divorce. Carla's mother already left! She took the convertible and drove back to Lexington."

"Horsefeathers," I muttered.

"Yeah," Maggie said, fidgeting with a long piece of straw. "Carla has been pretty rotten to us lately, but I wouldn't wish divorce on my worst enemy."

We were quiet for a minute. I was remembering how great Carla had been to me when I thought I was losing Orphan and the barn and everything I cared about. Maybe that's how she was feeling now. "Did Carla go with her mother?" I asked.

"Nope," Maggie answered. "I guess Carla's dad is already asking around for a housekeeper to stay with her when he's away on business. Can you believe it? I can't imagine staying with any of my fathers."

Jen hadn't said anything, but I could tell she wanted to. "What, Jen? What are you thinking?"

"Nothing," she said slowly. "I mean, I didn't know anything about the divorce until Maggie called. And I feel as sorry for Carla as you two do. But practically speaking ... what do you think this means for us? For Horsefeathers?"

"What do you mean, for Horsefeathers?" I asked.

"Well," Jen began, "I was just thinking that maybe this changes things for us. What about Ham now? Mrs. Buckingham didn't take the horse back with her, right?"

"Wow!" Maggie cried. "Jen, you are such a

businesswoman! Why didn't I think of that?"

I had no idea what they were getting at. "Think of what?" I demanded.

"Don't you get it, Scoop?" Maggie asked. "Mrs. Buckingham was the one who wanted Ham switched to Dalton Stables. So maybe now *Mr.* Buckingham will leave the horse here. Sometimes during a divorce, one spouse does exactly the opposite of what the other spouse planned to do, just to make them mad! The stories I could tell you about Husband #2!"

"Maggie!" Jen scolded. She turned to me. "You know, Scoop, Mr. Buckingham *did* like the way Ham looked. You said he thought Ham's coat was shiny. Besides, in all the hassle of a divorce, there's a chance Ham might get forgotten and they'll just leave him here."

A glimmer of hope ignited in me. Ham might get to stay at Horsefeathers. Then I felt guilty for thinking about myself instead of what Carla must be going through. "I don't feel right talking about it like this," I said. I wished Carla and I hadn't been on such horrible terms. As far as I knew, she didn't have a friend in the world—including her horse.

Meow! The Horsefeathers mascot brushed against my leg, demanding attention.

"She's adorable!" Maggie squealed, bending down to pet the cat's orange head. "I just wish I'd been here when Travis delivered her!"

I felt relieved to have the subject changed from the Buckinghams. "Not only is this cat adorable, she's smart. She's been helping me bake chocolate chip cookies. This morning she got so close to Ham I was afraid he'd step on her."

"Don't worry, Scoop," Jen said. "She'd still have eight lives left."

As if the cat understood us, she bounded to the paddock. We peeked through the stall window and watched her trot straight to Ham and weave between his forefeet.

"I almost forgot!" Maggie cried again. "Wait 'til you see what I brought!" She pulled a tape out of her pocket and popped it in the boom box. "It's *Cats!* You know, the Broadway musical."

I turned down the volume so we could still hear each other talk.

"So what's the cat's name?" Maggie asked.

Jen shrugged. "Whatever we want, I guess."

For the next 10 minutes we took turns making fun of every cat name we could think of—Cat, Kitty, Tabby, Sparkle, Tiger, and on and on.

"Hey down there!" I recognized B.C's voice, but I didn't see him. I figured he must have been eavesdropping on us from the barn roof. He hollered through a crack in the hayloft. "Why don't you call her Dogless?"

"Does he mean Douglas?" Jen asked.

"No!" Maggie said, laughing hysterically. "*Dog*-less! I love it, B.C.!" she yelled up. "Dogless it is! Dogless Cat."

~~~~~~~~~~~~~~~~~~~~~~~~~~~~~~

After Jen and Maggie left, I sat on the floor of Ham's stall and finished reading *Man O' War* while hymns played softly from B.C.'s player. Ham inched closer and closer, his ears flicking toward me, his eyes darting to me, then away again. I heard him at the stall door, and it was all I could do not to go over to him. He came so close I could smell him. I kept reading aloud as Dogless curled up in the feeding trough and purred.

When I left for the day, Dogless perched on top of the doorpost, rubbing from nose to tail against Ham's cheek. Ham stretched out his neck and shut his eyes.

~~~~~~~~~~~~~~~~~~~~~~~~~~~~~~

Back home, Grandad was no longer *home*, but I told him about the day's progress anyway. As I talked, he stared unblinking at a TV game show.

The next morning I got to Horsefeathers before the sun had climbed barn-high. Purple cloud smudges covered the sky like angelic fingerprints. I greeted Orphan and gave her a carrot, which she waved at me as she chomped.

Ham wasn't in his pasture. Instantly my

peaceful mood evaporated. Maybe Ham had jumped the fence again. Maybe he'd gotten tangled in Dalton's wire, the electricity turned on this time. Maybe Mrs. Buckingham had come in the night and taken her horse off to Kentucky.

I raced into the barn and stopped still. I had to bite my lip to keep from shouting. Ham was standing in his own stall, munching hay. And curled up on his back was Dogless Cat. *Thank You, God*, I prayed inside. I felt tears form behind my eyes, and I blinked them back.

I fed Ham Jen's special feed. He ate it fast, keeping one eye on me. His body language said he was ready to bolt at a moment's warning. When he was almost done, I got out one of the stable toys, a big, red, plastic beachball. I tossed the ball on the stable floor. Dogless leaped off Ham's back and pounced on the ball, pushing it out to the paddock.

Ham followed Dogless out, watching his stable buddy intently. A few more pounces, and the ball rolled to Ham's feet. Ham nosed it, and it rolled away, making him toss his head. His curiosity turned to playfulness. I joined in the party and kicked the ball into his pasture. Ham pranced up to it. Then he pushed it with his nose, snorting when it moved away from him.

Just after noon I brought in my final temptation—a long, green watermelon rind. (Hy-Klas had a special on watermelons.) It proved too much for Ham to resist. He stepped toward me as if his hooves were touching hot coals. Stretching his neck as far out as he could, he moved his lips until he touched the rind. Big, white teeth chomped half of the watermelon rind with one bite. He waved it in the air like a flag, proud of himself for making the grab.

By the time he finished the first half of the sweet, juicy rind, Ham was hooked. This time when he stepped toward me, I held my half of the rind closer to my body. Nearer and nearer he ventured. When he could reach the rind, he took a bite, but I held onto the rest, making him savor a small bite at a time. He finished eating out of my hand while I stroked his neck under his mane.

"Chocolate chip cookies," I said, draping my arm over Ham's broad back and leaning into him. He leaned back. I closed my eyes and rested my cheek against his side. "I hope you don't leave, Ham," I murmured. "I'd really miss having you around."

Buckingham's British Pride let me lunge him on the long line, trotting, walking, and cantering in circles to my voice commands. He didn't give me a lick of trouble when I saddled and bridled him and rode him through the pasture. I could hardly wait to get back and tell Grandad.

And I owed it all to Grandma Coop's secret recipe.

I finished chores and said good-bye to Orphan. All the way home, no matter how hard I tried to stop it, that spark of hope grew to a flame. If Mrs. Buckingham really had gone back to Lexington, then Jen was right. There was a good chance Ham could stay where he was— with Orphan and me at Horsefeathers. With time, Carla would come around too. Some of the worry weight that had pressed down on me for days began to break off.

The mail was sitting on the front porch, so I grabbed it on the way in. A long, white envelope caught my eye. My name and address were typed on the front. There was no return address, but the postmark said West Salem.

I ripped it open and unfolded the fancy, watermarked stationery:

Ms. Sarah Coop
Horsefeathers Stables

Dear Ms. Coop:

Enclosed you will find the balance due for the monthly boarding fee for Buckingham's British Pride. This letter is to inform you that we are terminating our agreement with Horsefeathers Stable. We will be picking up our horse and tack on the first and transferring to Dalton Stables.

Please have the horse ready by 9:00.

Regards,
Edward Buckingham III,
Attorney-at-Law

22

I phoned Maggie and Jen and told them about the letter from Carla's dad. Maggie burst into tears, but since I couldn't see through the phone lines, I didn't know if they were real tears or not. Jen didn't mean to, but she made me feel worse. She said she didn't see how we would ever make next month's bank payment.

Grandad had gone back inside himself and didn't say a word during supper. He just kept pressing his fork into his instant mashed potatoes and studying the little gray lines it made in the too-smooth lump of white. Dotty tried to carry on a cheery conversation by herself, but I saw her mouth tighten each time she asked Grandad a question he didn't answer.

After supper, B.C. escaped to the roof with a bag full of bottle caps. If he hadn't gotten there first, I might have spent some roof time myself. I had so much to think over—Ham, Carla, Horse-feathers, everything.

I tried to read, tried to think, tried to plan, but nothing worked. Part of me wanted to phone Carla, but I couldn't think of what to say. Finally, I flipped through some of the pages in Grandad's old photo album and went to bed early. That night I dreamed about a young girl in an old-fashioned dress and a young man who couldn't keep his eyes off her.

~~~~~~~~~~~~~~~~~~~~~~~~~~~~~~

In the morning at breakfast, I kept sneaking peeks at Dotty, trying to see the young girl from the photo somewhere inside my aunt. The girl was there, in Dotty's chin and in her eyes.

I got the photo album and opened it to the right picture—Dotty and her fiancé. "Dotty," I said, "who's this in the picture with you?"

Dotty wiped her hands on the dish towel and lumbered over to the table. She squinted down at the photo, then lowered herself into the chair beside me. Grinning, she pulled the scrapbook in front of her. "I forgot about that picture," she said.

She didn't say anything for a few seconds, and I felt like I was intruding on something. "That's Beauregard McCray," she said. "Bo."

"He was really handsome," I said, feeling stupid as soon as I said it.

"He was at that," she said.

She wasn't going to tell me more, and suddenly it seemed important for me to know, to understand. "Grandad said you were engaged. What happened? I mean, if you don't ... if it doesn't ... "

174

"Well, Scoop, I messed it up," she said, still staring at Bo.

"You?" I said. In the back of my mind, I'd figured it had to be the handsome Bo who had broken the engagement.

Dotty sighed. "I was engaged to Bo when I fell for another fella out of Kennsington. Met him in the bowling alley and thought it was love at first sight."

"Horsefeathers!" I said.

"I went riding with this new fella in his cherry red convertible up to Lover's Point and let him kiss me. Word got back to Bo and that was that."

"Dotty!" I couldn't have been more shocked if she'd told me Bo was from Mars. "I can't imagine you doing something like that!"

"I haven't always knowed the Lord, Scoop. It was after this, not long after, I became a Christian. Lucky for me, Jesus loves even sinners. So even if Bo didn't forgive me, Jesus did—washed me clean with His grace." She winked at me.

"What happened to the other guy?" I asked.

"Oh, he was gone as fast as he come. And a good thing too from what I heard tell after. Bo had went off to college—we was both gonna go. Then my daddy—and your mama's daddy—took sick. I stayed on to care for him.

"What about Bo? Didn't you ever talk to him again?"

Dotty tilted the scrapbook so his photo caught

more light. "I seen Bo two years back. He's a dentist in Kennsington. Got himself a real pretty wife and three growed kids." She set the scrapbook back down. "He still looks just like this here picture."

Dotty looked at me and laughed. "You look like you just discovered you was living with an alien."

"I'm sorry, Dotty," I said. "It's just ... well, I thought I knew all about you. Want to know something funny? The other day I was thinking that I was the only one who understood you. But I didn't—not like I thought I did. The same thing happened with me and Grandad in church. When I saw him directing that classical music, it was like this whole other side to him that I hadn't understood."

"People ain't never so easy to understand, Scoop," Dotty said.

"And Carla," I went on. "I thought I had her figured out too. She was just jealous of her new sister or brother. But now I'm not so sure that's it, Dotty. I'm not sure of anything."

Dotty pushed herself up from the table. "That ain't such a bad place to be, Honey," she said. "God's the only One who understands. The sooner we figure that out, the better."

She poured a cup of coffee and mumbled something.

"What did you say, Dotty?" I asked, putting the milk back in the fridge.

"Hmm?" she said, wiping up the counter.

"Oh, I'm just saying over that there verse you copied for me in church, still trying to get it into my head: *Lean not on your own understanding; in all your ways acknowledge Him, and ... and ...* For the life of me, I can't recollect what comes next."

"*And He will make your paths straight?*" I asked, the rest of the verse having stuck in my brain without being invited. *Make your paths straight.* I said it over in my head. I could sure use some path-straightening. I had no idea what to do about Ham—and even less of an idea what to do about Carla.

"That's it!" Dotty said. "*And He will make your paths straight!* That's what it's all about anyway, God's grace coming in and fixin' things we can't. Don't know why I can't get that part into my thick skull. Ain't you smart for remembering, Scoop!"

"I don't feel very smart, Dotty," I said. "I thought it was everybody else who didn't understand, who didn't have horse sense. Turns out it's me."

Dotty swiped her whole face with her apron, then smiled at me, showing the chipped tooth she never got time or money to get fixed. A faraway look in her eyes for just an instant made her look exactly like the young girl in the picture. It gave me goosebumps.

"Dotty—" I started, but I didn't know what to say. Maybe if she hadn't had to take care of me and B.C. all these years, maybe she'd have gotten married and had kids of her own.

Dotty reached out and took my hand. "Dontcha look like that, all sad and bothered, Scoop! I'm exactly where the Good Lord brung me and I wouldn't change with nobody. Not with nobody in the whole entire world, you understand?"

Understand. There was that word again. "If I do understand, Dotty, it's about the only thing I understand."

"Well, Honey," she said, hugging me, "That's a good place to start. It just might keep you from leaning too hard on your own understanding. Then you can lean on *His* understanding."

I shut my eyes and let Dotty's soft, thick arms spread around me. I imagined I was being hugged by the young Dotty in the picture. Then in my mind she transformed into her sister, my mom. Tears rolled down my cheeks and onto her arm. I tried to muffle the sobs, swallowing them until my throat burned.

I pulled away, keeping my head down so she couldn't see my face. "I better go spend some time with Ham," I said. "It looks like Dalton Stables will be coming for him tomorrow."

Dotty started to quiz me, but the phone rang. "I'll get it," she said, heading for the living room.

I dumped my cereal in the sink and started to leave. I had one hand on the kitchen screen door when I heard something in Dotty's voice that made me stop and eavesdrop.

"What?" she said into the receiver. "No, Sir. I'm sure."

I could see her wrapping the phone cord around her finger, something she only did for bad news. "Well, of course. I'll ask her," Dotty said. "Scoop?"

I felt in my stomach it was something terrible. My hand froze on the latch.

Dotty walked as far as the receiver let her and hollered into the kitchen at me. "Scoop? You ain't seen Carla this morning, have you?"

"Carla?" I repeated stupidly. "I haven't seen her since the horse show, Dotty."

Dotty lumbered back to the living room. "Mr. Buckingham, Sir, Scoop ain't seen your daughter." She was quiet, then answered, "Now, now, I ain't saying Scoop's perfect, but she ain't lying. 'Sides, I'd of seen your girl if she come by the house. Now don't you worry none about— Hello? Hello?" Dotty stared at the receiver, then hung up.

I'd been squeezing the screen door handle so hard my palm ached. I let it go. "What did Mr. Buckingham want?"

Dotty leaned in the doorway, one hand on the wall. "That poor man, Scoop. He is beside hisself. Good Lord, take care of that daddy and show him Your peace." She switched back to talking to me again as natural as if God and Dotty and me had been having us a three-way conversation. "Scoop, I think that little girl's run away."

23

"Carla Buckingham ran away?" I stared at Dotty. "And her dad thought she came here? I don't understand."

Dotty grinned. "So you pray while you run look for her at Horsefeathers, hear? God will help you understand. Now git!"

~~~~~~~~~~~~~~~~~~~~~~~~~~~~~~~~~

I ran as fast as I could until my side felt like knives were stabbing me. The minute I turned into the lane, I heard my name. "Scoop!" Travis came running toward me. I saw his white pickup parked under the maple tree.

I kept walking, and Travis and I met in the lane. "We were just about to come get you, Scoop!" Travis said, taking my arm and pulling me toward the barn.

I spotted Jen. She waved her arms at us, like a ringmaster calling the horses in from the ring.

"What is it?" I asked as I jogged to the barn next to Travis, his hand still holding my arm.

"Ham's gone," Travis said. "And Jen said his saddle and bridle are gone too."

"Travis was just going to drop me off so I could ride Cheyenne," Jen said. "But we heard meowing and crying."

"And I knew it was that cat," Travis said.

"Dogless," Jen said. "So we looked for her and found her alone in Ham's stall."

Travis finished their story. "And we couldn't find Ham anywhere. He's really gone, Scoop."

"Carla's gone too," I said.

Jen and Travis exchanged looks. "You don't think they're—You don't think she—" Jen couldn't get the words out, but that's exactly what I was already thinking, what we were all thinking. Carla had run away on Ham.

Orphan whinnied, a shrill, demanding call. She had trotted along the fence, keeping pace in the paddock as I ran up the lane. Now she demanded my attention.

"I'll take Orphan and look for Carla and Ham," I said.

While I fetched a rope, I told Travis and Jen about the call from Mr. Buckingham. I tied each end of the rope to Orphan's halter for a crude rein. Travis gave me a boost up. "If Carla's half as upset as her dad," I said, feeling my horse under me, ready to go, "then Ham is going to pick up on it. I don't know what that horse might do to Carla if he freaks out again."

"Take Travis with you," Jen said. "Ham could be wild. And Carla could really get hurt. I'll go for help. I'll call Mr. Buckingham. Can you ride double, Travis?"

"I guess I'm game if Scoop is," Travis said. "Is it okay with Orphan, Scoop?"

"Okay," I said, scooting forward as far as I could, until I was right over Orphan's withers. B.C. and I had ridden double a couple of times, and Orphan was plenty big enough to carry Travis and me.

"Travis," I said, "go stand on the mounting stump. I'll ride Orphan over so you can get on." I rode as close to the tree stump as I could, and Travis slid in behind me.

"Easy, Orphan," I said, as Travis put his arms around my waist. "Easy, Girl." I was really saying it to myself more than to Orphan. Travis' arms were barely touching me, but I still couldn't breathe.

"All set," Travis announced.

I was thankful Orphan seemed to know what to do without me. She circled to the front gate. Jen held it open and we rode through. "Good luck!" Jen called. "I'll get help!"

Orphan headed toward the woods behind Buckinghams'. She broke to a canter, and Travis clung to me. His chin was just above my head, and his mouth was so close to my ear I could feel his breath. "I think Orphan knows where Ham went," he said.

Orphan took a shortcut across the stream, splashing us to the knees. She raced up a hill to the clearing that led to the woods. Light softened inside the pines, and I saw shadows everywhere until I couldn't trust what I was seeing.

"Why do you think Carla ran away?" Travis asked. "She's got everything a kid could want. Guess you never really know about a person, do you?"

I shook my head and couldn't think of an answer for him. *Dear God*, I prayed, *I don't understand Carla, but I want to. I need Your understanding. Whatever's going on with Carla, keep her safe and let us find her and Ham. Make our path straight.*

I could have sworn I said my whole prayer inside my head, but when I was done, I heard Travis whisper, "Amen."

"There!" Travis yelled. "I think I see her. Down there!"

Orphan trotted off the path, so close to a white pine I heard the bristles hit Travis.

Then I saw her. Carla was on the ground, lying curled up and facing away from us.

"Carla!" I screamed. "Carla!" I slid off Orphan and ran to her. "Are you hurt? Don't move."

She was crying, her whole body shaking. I glanced at Travis, who was on the ground now,

holding Orphan's reins. He stayed back and nodded to me.

"Hold still. Jen sent for help, Carla," I said.
"Is anything broken? I know what you're going
through—"

She turned and glared at me. "You don't
know anything! You have no idea." Her eyes had
so much pain in them I could almost feel it. She
sat up, and at least it didn't look like she'd broken anything. But something inside her had broken. I prayed again for understanding.

"Go away!" she screamed.

"Carla, we know your parents are getting
divorced. Let me help you. I want to understand."

She turned away. "You don't understand
anything. Nobody understands," she mumbled.

"That's not true, Carla," I said softly. "*I*
don't understand—you're right about that. But
Jesus does understand. He's the only One who
does. He suffered everything on earth so He
could understand."

I closed my eyes and let my heart pray to
God for help, for understanding. There was
something more to all of this, something I was
missing.

And then I knew. I don't know how I knew
or why, but I understood. "You're not going to
have a brother or sister, are you, Carla?"

She wheeled around as if I'd shot her, but

the anger left her eyes and let me into their pure, agonizing pain. "My mother ... She had an abortion. I *had* a sister or a brother, Scoop. And now I don't."

I couldn't see her face anymore because my own eyes were tear-blurred. The air seemed dense as pond water, and there were no sounds in the forest. It felt exactly as if somebody had died.

We held on to each other and sobbed. I pictured the sister or brother who would never know Carla and who Carla would never know—but never ever forget. I wanted to scream. I wanted to go backwards in time and stop it.

Carla whispered, "Mother moved back to Lexington. I've lost a family, Scoop."

I didn't know what to say. I knew she'd see her mother again. She hadn't really lost her, not like I'd lost mine. But I still had my brother, and she'd never get hers back. I wished B.C. could have been there so I could tell him how glad I was that I had him for a brother.

I don't know how long we stayed like that, holding on to each other, rocking back and forth. When we ran out of tears and I felt as if somebody had wrung out my heart, I heard a nicker. I looked up to see Travis standing alone. He pointed a few yards away. Orphan was standing next to Ham, their necks stretched over each other's backs in a horse hug.

I nudged Carla and pointed to the horses. "Look at them, Carla. They're starting over. I think Orphan understands Ham now. She's got a lot of horse sense."

"Scoop," she said, staring at the horses, "do you think Ham will ever forgive me for the way I've treated him?"

"I'm sure of it," I said. "Ham's got a lot of horse sense too."

I helped Carla to her feet. Nothing seemed broken, not even bruised. She'd landed in soft, brown pine needles that cushioned her fall, leaving only a few tiny scratches. They'd heal. I prayed that the rest of her would heal too.

Travis walked us back to Horsefeathers while the horses followed quietly behind, the padding of their hooves the only sound in the woods. I didn't know how much Travis had overheard, but I liked him a lot for not asking questions.

Dogless met us in the pasture and tiptoed back with us right next to Ham. When we got to the barn, Mr. Buckingham ran up to us. "Carla, are you okay?" he asked, hugging her. "I am so sorry, Honey. I had no idea how upset you were. We'll work this out together. You can help me understand."

Carla hugged him back. And I prayed God would give them the understanding they'd need to put their lives back together.

24

The next morning when the Dalton Stables trailer showed up at Horsefeathers, we were all there waiting for them. Maggie and Moby, and Jen and Cheyenne formed our front line of defense. Behind them stood Ray and Travis, followed by Carla and Orphan and me.

Mr. Buckingham met Ralph Dalton and shook his hand. Stephen and Ursula stepped out of the trailer cab. "We're here for your horse, Mr. Buckingham. I hope everything's in order," said Ralph Dalton.

"I don't believe so," said Mr. Buckingham.

"Excuse me?" said Ralph Dalton, his bushy eyebrows dipping to form a V.

"I don't believe Carla's horse is ready for Dalton Stables," Mr. Buckingham said evenly.

Ursula whispered to Stephen so loud I didn't have any trouble hearing it. "He's *not* thinking of leaving his horse here, is he?" she asked.

The barn door slapped open, like a single clap at the end of a performance. B.C., his hands behind his back, threaded through our defensive line until he reached Stephen and Ursula. Dramatically, he produced from behind his back one of his bottle cap creations, a kind of mini-cage.

"Go away, B.C.!" Stephen said. He whispered something about my brother that made Ursula giggle.

"What *is* that thing?" she said, bending over the cage and looking down her long, slim nose at B.C.'s creation.

B.C. moved the cage closer. "I call it Spider in a Cage," he said, opening the door.

Ursula screamed and ran back to the trailer. Stephen followed her, wiggling and brushing himself as if he were covered with baby spiders.

"That's my brother!" I said proudly. He turned and grinned back at me.

"See here, Buckingham! You're making a big mistake," said Ralph Dalton.

"Mr. Dalton," said Edward Buckingham, III, putting his arm around his daughter's shoulders, "I've made a lot of mistakes. This is not one of them. Good day."

We cheered as they drove away. Carla, Maggie, Jen, and I took the horses on a great, long ride. After we'd turned them out to pasture together, Carla and I met Dotty at my house. Clouds gathered fast and dumped hard rain on the dried land in a fury of thunder and lightning.

When the rain let up, Dotty drove Carla,

B.C., and me to the cemetery, where we put up a small, white cross right next to the two graves of the babies of Emma and Benjamin Coop. Dotty slipped her arm around Carla. "Lord, our hearts hurt just like we know Your heart hurts. One of Your precious babies was killed. We ask You to put Your arm around Carla's mama and help her understand that she took a life You created. Help us show her that Jesus died to pay for our sin, no matter how awful. And He rose so we could live forever in heaven with Him." Dotty sounded so hopeful that some of her peace seemed to pass on to Carla.

I knew Carla would never completely get over her losses any more than I'd "gotten over" losing my folks in the explosion. There were so many things about people and life I'd never understand. But God understood, and maybe Carla and I were beginning to understand each other.

As we walked back to Horsefeathers to tell our horses goodnight, the clouds pulled back like billowing curtains. We looked up into the sky at a gold-rimmed window of sunshine. Light streamed from behind the clouds as if God were peeking out at us from the heavens through a pocket of grace.

Glossary of Gaits

Gait—A gait is the manner of movement, the way a horse goes.

There are four natural or major gaits most horses use: walk, trot, canter, and gallop.

Walk—In the walk, the slowest gait, hooves strike the ground in a four-beat order: right hind hoof, right fore hoof, left hind hoof, left fore hoof.

Trot—In the trot, hooves strike the ground in diagonals in a one-two beat: right hind and left forefeet together, left hind and right forefeet together.

Canter—The canter is a three-beat gait containing an instant during which all four hooves are off the ground. The foreleg that lands last is called the "lead" leg and seems to point in the direction of the canter.

Gallop—The gallop is the fastest gait. If fast enough, it's a four-beat gait, with each hoof landing separately: right hind hoof, left hind hoof just before right fore hoof, left fore hoof.

Other gaits come naturally to certain breeds or are developed through careful breeding.

Running walk—This smooth gait comes naturally to the Tennessee Walking Horse. The horse glides between a walk and a trot.

Pace—A two-beat gait, similar to a trot. But instead of legs pairing in diagonals as in the trot, fore and hindlegs on one side move together, giving a swaying action.

Slow gait—Four beats, but with swaying from side to side and a prancing effect. The slow gait is one of the gaits used by Five-Gaited Saddle Horses. Some call this pace the stepping pace or amble.

Amble—A slow, easy gait, much like the pace.

Rack—One of the five gaits of the Five-Gaited American Saddle Horse, it's a fancy, fast walk. This four-beat gait is faster than the trot and is very hard on the horse.

Jog—A jog is a slow trot, sometimes called a **dogtrot**.

Lope—A slow, easygoing canter, usually referring to a Western gait on a horse ridden with loose reins.

Fox trot—An easy gait of short steps in which the horse basically walks in front and trots behind. It's a smooth gait, great for long-distance riding and characteristic of the Missouri Fox Trotter.

About the Author

Dandi Daley Mackall rode her first horse—bareback—when she was 3. She's been riding ever since. She claims some of her best friends have been horses she and her family have owned: mixed-breeds, quarter horses, American Saddle Horses, Appaloosas, Pintos, and Paints.

When she isn't riding, Dandi is writing. She has published more than 200 books for children and adults, including *The Cinnamon Lake Mysteries* and *The Puzzle Club Mysteries*, both for Concordia. Dandi has written for *Western Horseman* and other magazines as well. She lives in rural Ohio, where she rides the trails with her husband Joe (also a writer), children Jen, Katy, and Dan, and the real Moby and Cheyenne (pictured below).